The Path To Awakening

THE SAD MIGRANT

Jesús Edgar Medina Adame

_jema_sid

Translated by _jema_sid
Translation contributions by Joel Jerez

Content

Behind My Eyes

My ignorance reaches
what my wisdom
cannot imagine.

_jema_sid

Excerpts from the prologue

Social injustice has become something that we have become accustomed to seeing as commonplace, and we have learned to deal with the idea in one way or another. Human beings recognize the faults and deficiencies that exist in this modern society, but nevertheless it does not seem to matter too much to us, as long as it does not affect the circle of conformity in which we live. According to what we experience around the planet, there does not seem to be any upcoming change to attend to the existential needs that overwhelm the population, rather it seems that the opposite is what is planned to be done, since the misinformation and lack of coherence with which it is intended to direct the new generations is merely an absurd mockery.

The tools necessary for spiritual growth are denied, and many times hidden to avoid at all costs that human beings can have free and safe access to these tools of order. The powerful do not want free and conscious people, they are only interested in the ignorant and slaves, that is why this specific machination is generated to deceive and control the world population.

The lack of employment and opportunities that exist in the poorest countries of our precious paradise, in addition to social injustice and uncontrolled crime, prompt the population to take drastic measures, by giving them no other option than to emigrate to lands with better opportunities. Corruption only promotes pain and discontent, which is why millions of people try to flee from the petty desire of the powerful, to try to give their loved ones a better life, even if it means risking their lives. Thousands manage to reach that opportunity, although not all take advantage of it in the best way by falling into the illogical vice of the lie of profit and fame, which ego and vanity create in their minds. Many of us know that reality is stranger than fantasy, so we do not blind ourselves to any possibility. Many may think that these are just absurd conspiracy beliefs to think that governments are corrupt and indifferent to the population and that they only want to manipulate us to continue with the control. If this were not the case, then the interest in helping would be evident, but it is not, because this interest in helping the poorest and most needy is not appreciated anywhere, to those who live under injustice and inequality. Anyone who tries to get ahead by helping the innocent is seen today as a phony, while corrupt liars and criminals are seen as heroes. Now the bad is apparently good, and the good is a joke. The systematic racism that is generated in the midst of confusing and absurd politics, has created aggressive ideological divisions against all those who do not fit into the social standards and models, which are dictated between lies and deceit by these corrupt manipulators. It is decency and good principles that should govern when playing with the fate of human beings, but unfortunately, that is not the case, thanks to these unscrupulous politicians who deceive their followers with meanness and false arguments about the truth. What kind of civilization is one that protects dogs more than human beings, just because of their skin color or the language they speak? Today they glory in power, but one day they will be just the shame of our past.

My awakening

One night I dreamed that I was born among green and blue feathers.

A lightning illuminated the abyss below the cloak that held my soul, then I came out into this world.

In the anthill are my feet swollen by bitterness and hate that pollute the water on this planet.

Sores my hands tear time, writing it between the stones.

Letting go of the cause that remains eternal in and out.

Thus, in the middle of the scene, my soul descends into the heart of heaven.

Receives it: Caculha- Huracan, Chipi-caculha, Raxa-caculha.

With the approval of: Tepeu and Gucumatz. In this beautiful world of life unique and essential.

_jema_sid

7/4/2011

_jema_sid

Chapter 1
A Unique Treasure

For Phillip it was a miracle to have received the award for best architectural design from Elida's grandmother's foundation. He did not know what to do with so much money because he had never had more than what he got by digging through the trash. Life in grandmother's mansion made him reflect on what he could do with the money.

Every weekend they went out to offer service to the community of the nearby towns, as was the custom in grandmother's mansion. It seemed as if there was nothing else that filled them with pride and satisfaction, especially for Chendo and his family.

Having lived among the humblest, they learned how important it is to help those who have almost nothing. That was why they even prepared for days for the weekend, to lend a hand in the same way that they would have liked someone to have done for them.

The children assimilated the same education inherited by the grandparents, with the example of mercy and the willingness to help without expecting anything in return. Phillip used the money to help several people from some towns in the district, despite the fact that he never received any comfort or help from many of those people. Either way, he rewarded them with money and some real estate for the home, for the lesson he learned when they wrongly looked down on him.

People never knew that the help they received was from that poorly dressed and misplaced beggar, who had once been kicked off the sidewalk of their houses just for looking inappropriate for their pride.

The determination and good principles in Phillip were clear, who received only discrimination and contempt from almost all those who always misjudged him. It takes a lot of character to forgive disrespect and aggression, especially emotional ones.

He is the silent and truthful example that teaches us not to hold grudges or hate, but to forgive and love even those who hate us. He always said, "Forgive those who don't know us, those who are lost and lack knowledge" That is to have a strong and wise heart, one of those that is very difficult to discover nowadays.

There is no doubt that good values are learned at home, regardless of the economic or social level in which one lives. There is no excuse or pretext that avoids good manners and respect. Whoever says otherwise is deceived and lost like a blind and deaf slave who does not want to live.

Early one Wednesday morning, Chendo accompanied Phillip and Raúl to deliver a new truck to Uicho as a reward for his loyalty, and for allowing his design to be built, with which he had won the award from the grandmother's architectural foundation, which took place every two years, and for which the best architects in the world competed.

The foundation prepared an event to recognize the winner of the award, in front of all the academics in the field, from all the universities in the country, and many more that belonged to universities in other world-class countries.

That was something that he had not seen in any of his visions, but that he was not unaware of knowing that he was capable of doing what any other man could.

Although there was something that did not leave him alone, and that was perhaps the doubt and the fear of not being appreciated as he wanted. Phillip did not want to attend because he felt overwhelmed by so many talented and well-recognized people, who would surely make fun of him, knowing the origin of where that design had come from, which everyone agreed was the best in its category.

Phillip insisted to the grandmother that he was already prepared for the recognition of his achievements, so no event was necessary, other than knowing that he had won something so prestigious and admired.

The grandmother insisted that it was necessary for everyone to know who he was, and to recognize him as a man capable of doing the same or better than all of them because he had earned it with his talent. "The answer is in your heart, my Quixote." Elida told him, while she watched him looking at the sunset, wondering if he would attend the event or not.

He was about to realize one of his most cherished dreams, at least as far as his personal aspirations as an earthly man are concerned.

It had become customary for everyone in the mansion to express their opinion about what was happening, because nothing was hidden, or someone was discriminated against because of their position or obligation in household chores, that is why everyone was present when Phillip was trying to reason if he wanted to attend the event or not. There was something that he sensed but that he could not define in his mind, something that tried to warn him about the beginning of a movement of specific energies, which defined his destiny in each decision and each step of his way.

Somehow, he knew that all of this was inevitable, that he could not oppose or deny what the divine had prepared for his path. Also, seeing everyone around the table, he felt that this was the moment he always dreamed of, and he did not want to lose that magic that he clung to every night.

He felt in his heart that those moments were the best of his life, and which he would miss when loneliness and sadness overwhelmed him. He wanted the moment to last forever, though he knew that was never the case.

Raúl talked with Chendo about some things that were needed to repair some of the mansion's walls, while Mama Chayo and the grandmother knitted some clothes for the children, who boasted of playing around.

The oldest of the three children was very attentive to what was happening, and with that innocence and spontaneity that characterized him, he told Phillip:

"One day I want to be like you."

Phillip stared at Elida, who was carrying her beloved daughter Emma in her arms, and then turned to look towards the window, where he could see the sunset, which welcomed him in yet another of its sublime indications.

In a certain way, he felt a little afraid, knowing beforehand the events that were taking place before his eyes. He knew that there was something else that he subconsciously wanted to avoid.

It was thanks to the support of the entire family that he decided to face his destiny with courage and without fear, knowing that anything was possible.

Besides that, he had earned it by his own merit, and by his talent. It was a completely opposite scenario to what he had always experienced, so he strove to keep vanity and ego out of his ideology to not confuse the example he was trying to pass on to his beloved daughter Emma and the children, who without a doubt could tell how proud they were of him.

He received a commemorative plaque from Dr. Ernesto Guevara for the achievement he had achieved with his design, before all the academics who rose from their seats to honor him with euphoric applause, which lasted for more than a minute and a half.

Phillip wholeheartedly appreciated the intention of respect and admiration with which they applauded him, but even so, he felt a little overwhelmed by the flatter and felt a great need to run out of that place.

He concentrated on his purpose in life, on what he represented to those who loved him, he could not lose himself in the vanity created for the moment. The great pride that Elida reflected at that moment made him immediately return to his convictions and purposes that he always kept in his heart. Phillip cried the moment he took Emma into his arms, along with the recognition he had received.

He went from being a mistreated and ignored beggar to being surrounded by prestigious academics who congratulated him personally, giving him the recognition he deserved for having created that masterpiece.

His knowledge and skill bore corresponding fruits. They showed him that in the right place and with the right people, his qualities were properly appreciated without envy or ignorance.

Next to the river, near the mansion, Phillip was pruning some grape vines thinking about what had happened, trying to specify the message that all this brought him.

Some laborers who worked near where Phillip was, were talking about one of their cousins, who had emigrated to another country in search of better opportunities. Phillip listened attentively, while they told others about how that man's life had changed after a while, because he was able to build his house and provide better economic well-being for his family, in just a few months.

I do not know if it is envy, or greed, or the poverty in which we live in the world, which encourages us to emigrate in search of a better future for those we love, despite sacrificing our lives in exchange for a sublime dream, which almost all of us strive to achieve.

Even before nations and kingdoms were created, we emigrated in search of better lands, where we felt we would not have a shortage of food or shelter for our families. There were no borders.

Some of those who were nearby heard that they were talking about the young man, so they approached to ask more about him, since he was someone they knew. They wanted to know if it was possible for them to also emigrate to the country where his friend had emigrated. They asked them how his friend had done to get to that country.

Phillip was amazed at the story that one of the young men told them about the adventure that his cousin had had when looking for his dream.

The young man recounted that when he arrived at the border his cousin had taken refuge along with four others in a place called San Francisquito, to wait for the *coyote* so that he would then take them illegally across the border. Because the laws of that country were based on banal principles, and interests that not many manage to understand, not allowing emigration out of necessity.

They demanded merits based on a model that segregated the poorest and discriminated against those of a certain appearance or skin color, for reasons that only their ignorance understood.

It is incredible that in this first world country dogs were allowed to enter, but not human beings. Now that is uncivilized. Each one judge in your own way.

They had walked for five days in the desert, when two began to weaken due to lack of food and water, for that reason they had to leave them under some bushes so they would not die so soon from the sun, and if by a miracle they regained the necessary forces, they could return as they could.

They continued walking despite the fact that they hardly had the strength to think anymore, until they reached a nearby hill, where they took refuge in a small cave to regain their strength. The young man felt that he was dying from the lack of water, so before entering the cave he fell next to a bush, with no strength in his body other than his hope.

Before losing consciousness, with one eye closed and the other half opened, he managed to notice the almost skeletal body of some man or woman lying under the bushes, who had suffered the same fate which he was about to experience. Luckily for him, that skeleton was holding a bottle with something to drink in one of the hands. With what little strength he drew from his will to live, he pulled the container from between the bones of the hand, which shattered the moment he pulled the bottle.

That pomegranate juice revived him, giving him enough strength to get up and walk into the cave, where the other three lay on the ground, unconscious from lack of water and food. He gave each one a couple of sips, which brought them back, after a few minutes of the nutrients in the pomegranate juice turning into rational thoughts and waking up again to the reality where they were on the brink of death., for pursuing an idea of prosperity, which is based solely on the material.

Each one thought about what they was leaving behind, with the exception of the *coyote*, who had already gone through some experiences but continued because of the good remuneration he obtained for passing them across the border. It was not that he did not care about his family, he also thought about his own, because this time he was about to lose his life. Each one judge in your own way.

After an hour and a half that they recovered the courage to continue, the *coyote* told them: "In a little while, we arrived at Casa Grande, and we did it." The boys drew strength from the memories of their loved ones, even though they thought they might never see them again, even so, they followed the *coyote* until they reached their goal.

Phillip had listened to the story that the young man said about his cousin's audacity to cross the border, in order to give his loved ones a better life; so, he went back to the mansion thinking very seriously about what he had heard.

It is not that he intended to do the same as those poor immigrants, risking their lives to try to achieve that uncertain dream, but rather to face his own destiny, in his own way and with his own means.

He believed that this was something very noble and admirable, trying to do what very few dared, despite risking their lives. Either way, he and his family were already doing it, risking their lives just to protect the truth.

At that moment, he had a presentiment about The Old Lady with the White Hair, and her advice on the path he should follow to reach the purpose that the divines had entrusted to him.

Of course, he knew that it was not about what he could obtain through wealth, but what the spirit could achieve, but even so, he was not entirely clear about the nature of his entire mission, and that made him confused at times.

If we were certain of everything that happens in life, we would have nothing to learn.

He stopped in the garden watching Elida, who was holding Emma in the middle of the roses, singing to her the same song that her mother had taught her as a child. He thought of giving them one of the roses, so he approached to cut one, but The Rose freed itself from the bush and fell on his hand, then one of the thorns pricked his ring fingertip.

At that moment, he had a vision of a world far away, which made him feel as if all this was just the beginning of what he felt in his heart. He knew he would have to be brave if he wanted to know more about his nature, about who he was. He approached them and placed The Rose on his beloved daughter Emma.

Elida looked at him with tenderness at the moment when a tear fell from Phillip's eyes, for which she touched his cheek very gently, and cried along with him, while he said to them, "For yah with all my heart."

At that moment Gabriel appeared from among the flowers in the garden and approached them, then he fell on his knees in front of Emma, bowing with respect, then stood up to embrace them and kissed Emma on the forehead. "Blessed is the fruit of your womb, and blessed is she among all women" Gabriel said to them, at the moment when he gave them the blessing. He gave Elida a bowl with a drink prepared to feed Emma, the time and day suggested by him, so that she would prepare herself in her way, which had been destined for her from the highest of creation.

He asked her to take Moonlight to her room so she could get some sleep because he had to talk to Phillip about some issues. Elida knew of the destiny that the divines had entrusted Phillip, and it did not surprise her that they visited him so that he could receive the necessary instruction for his task. She prepared to return to the mansion.

Mama Chayo was waiting for her at the door to take Emma and take her with her inside her so that she could sleep a little, between kisses and caresses all the time on the way to her room.

Phillip walked for half an hour next to Gabriel in the garden, listening to his advice on what he should do to protect those he loved from the evil that ruled this world, because they would persecute them no matter where they took refuge to kill them and continue hiding the truth.

Perhaps it is not entirely clear for many to think that governments keep us submerged in lies, and many still have no idea what the truth means because petty suggestion has been successful to deceive and dominate with false promises to the population. Every day it is more difficult to spread the message as there are no people willing to receive it.

He felt an immense desire to renounce the designs he had on his back, and he touched his belly with both hands because of the sensation he felt, at the moment when Gabriel placed his right hand on his forehead.

"The truth is in your heart," Gabriel told him.

He also told him that the decision of what he should do would come at the right time, therefore he should pay attention to not fall into the deception that clouds our hearts when responding to the concerns that await in it. That each one would receive the message in their own way, and that it was necessary for each one to assimilate it in the best way, to achieve a reunion with themselves.

After Gabriel left, Phillip returned to the mansion, thoughtful and worried about not knowing what he should do to guarantee the well-being of those he loved.

He had to talk to grandmother after having discussed a few things with his beloved Elida, about what he should do to achieve the impossible exploit of leaving a better world for his daughter Emma. The grandmother was happy to hear that he wanted to seek his life in his own way, wanting to find out what his destiny had for him elsewhere. She told him that this was a very noble thing of him, to count on her for whatever he needed.

Phillip told her a little about what he had heard in the vineyard about the brave man, who had crossed the border to look for a better future for his family, risking his life to be able to give them a certain comfort of goods and services.

The Grandmother interrupted him, telling him not to worry about it, that he did not have to risk anyone's life, because she would take care of getting them a visa to cross the border legally. That thanks to the prize he had won, he would not have to fight to get a permit to live in that country, to which Phillip planned to emigrate with his family.

The prize money was enough for him to stay and live a quiet life in this place, but he knew he would have to fly with his own wings if he wanted to raise his family. He made sure to save enough to sustain himself for a few months, the rest

16

he used to create two foundations to help children in marginalized communities with food and clothing; In addition, to establish a school near where the dump was located, so that the children would have the opportunity to educate themselves enough, to not be so easily deceived by the abusers.

He was trying to give them the chance he never had, freeing them from the ignorance and fear that prevented their dreams from growing. In this way, he was able to fulfill his dream, which at some point he thought was impossible, but now he did not mind giving everything to make it come true.

He made sure to create the right environment so that everything was self-sustaining in a certain way, thanks to the great skill that Elida and he had, to visualize what was convenient and appropriate at each administrative, architectural, and environmental point.

Each foundation had parcels around the central offices, designed by Phillip and Raúl, the grandmother's driver.

Raúl and the grandmother were great friends, in the same way, that Raúl was with Elida's grandfather. Almost everything Raúl knew about architecture he had learned from him; in the many years they shared together.

Raúl told Phillip that he had come to love Elida's grandfather like a brother.

The legumes that were harvested in both foundations were sold in nearby towns, and they used the profits to help the neediest communities in the region, with basic goods and services; thus, the promotion of good intra-family education, mutual respect, and towards nature.

Phillip tried to recreate a little piece of that paradise that he remembered on occasions, that even his compadre Chendo reminded him of when together they planted the last tree in The Southern Foundation.

The grandmother, Elida, and Emma, everyone from the mansion were there, celebrating such a great intention to help. That even the grandmother contributed to make it a little bigger than what Phillip had considered; for which, he did not object in the least, since the example had come from her, to give and help without any interest in return, just as he felt in his heart.

He felt more and more that he was leaving the legacy that he always wanted, thanks to the contributions that grandmother made so that everything was done in the best way, in addition to the support of his entire family. Everyone in the mansion, because in his heart they were all his family.

One night on a new moon, Phillip went with Chendo and Raúl, in the truck they used to take things to towns, to rescue the last things from his hat, without the evil leaders realizing anything, because they arrived by the place where hardly anyone goes at night. Except for Phillip and Chendo, who sometimes spent their time in that place at night watching the moon rise.

The hut was intact, as when they left it that day when they had to flee. The leaders did not even realize that they had not been there all that time, because of the little importance they had for them; Furthermore, not even the neighbors bothered to see what had happened to them. And no one ever knew that Phillip had earned a great fortune, nor that the help that came to the community was from Elida and Phillip.

The three trunks his father had inherited, along with a hundred boxes filled with almost every kind of rare item; also some things that Chendo managed to rescue from what was left of his hat, because his hat was in a noticeable place so people took advantage of the fact that it was alone and looted it, leaving only a few photographs and personal things, which had no value to anyone, but for Chendo they represented his most valuable treasure.

In the end they almost filled the truck with everything they took out. Phillip noticed that some of his plants had grown again, and he asked Raúl and Chendo to remove them with the care and manner suggested by him so that the plants would not suffer.

He noticed that something was moving in the water of the well where he had the fish, so he was greatly surprised to see that three of them had survived, so they were immediately thrown into buckets of water to take them to the mansion. Everything that had a sentimental value he took with him, so nothing could be left for those corrupts and ignorant misers. At the end of having uploaded his great treasure to the truck, it was hard for him to say goodbye to all the memories he had of his parents, so he cried silently knowing that he would move away from the place where they lived for a long time.

With his mind and thoughts, he told them that he loved them, and that he missed them very much. He heartily told them that he would see them again soon and that he would do whatever was necessary to honor them in this life.

Chendo told him that it was time to go, when Phillip was lost among the memories of him staring at the orchard where his mother taught him to live.

Phillip asked Raúl to take him near the cave because he wanted to leave some things that he would not need in his future plans, knowing that no one could find them in that place. No matter how hard they try to find the physical location of the door, they will fail in their search, or it will become a wrong search. This is so if one intends to search for the nature of the spirit in the external world.

They left the trunk of that Irish galleon in the cave, along with the pectoral and the medallion, as well as the letters from the Queen of England to the President of that nation.

He left the watch that his father had left him, just above the photo where his parents were in the square of one of the nearby towns.

Because of the wise advice he had received from Gabriel, in the mansion's garden, and because of what he had already sensed in his heart, he took the book with him, hidden inside his backpack. Raúl and his compadre Chendo saw him put it in his backpack, but they did not say a single word about it, because they thought it was one more of the many mysterious books of his that had been put on the truck.

Everyone in the mansion was filled with amazement at the things Phillip had collected from the trash.

Elida did not stop showing her grandmother of every little find, who was amazed to see all those relics that had great monetary and historical value. It took days to order and catalog all the things that Phillip had, since all kinds of rare objects and unrelated vessels made it difficult to assign them a certain utility or purpose. The books managed to fill the library, which even the grandmother asked Raúl to build one more shelf because there were still uncatalogued books.

Raúl, along with Elida's help, formed a list to evaluate item by item, and to be able to determine its value more easily.

Some things were donated to the country's national museum because they were relevant to history, but others Phillip and the grandmother had decided to keep, at the suggestion of Raúl, who was an excellent connoisseur of art, and who also had a doctorate in archaeology.

The grandmother and Raúl took Phillip and Elida to a place where there was a hidden vault, where they kept rare objects of incalculable value so that they could keep their belongings that they had decided to keep for the future.

The place was unsuspected, no one would ever realize where it was, so Phillip trusted to leave his most valuable belongings in the family vault.

After Raúl advised him to sell some things, and after having discussed it with Elida in their night talks, he decided to sell what he gave a different value to what most people give to things, and he used the money to further strengthen the foundations and the school they had formed.

"Good deeds attract good people," Phillip said, since many good people joined the cause that he set with the example of The Southern Foundation and The Atlantic Foundation, in addition, of The School of Mystery.

Mormon missionaries and members of different religious denominations came together to build new homes next to the dump, to form a new community with the basic services necessary for a dignified life.

They formed streets and housing lots with heavy machinery, where hundreds of good-hearted people volunteered to build houses, for each one of those who lived in the dump. Everything was financed by Phillip and the grandmother, the materials, and the machinery, thanks to the money he raised from the sale of some of his things, which he had taken from that place. This was the moment to use it to make that dream that he had for a long time come true, and that did not seem like it would ever end.

With the help of the authorities, they managed to unmask the abusive leaders, without them realizing that Phillip was behind it all.

Thanks to the fall of these corrupt abusers, it was that they managed to rescue many pieces that they had stolen from some archaeological excavations near that place, which were sold on the black market at a very high value.

All the people who lived in the dump were crying, thanking the state mission officers, together with the municipal officials, for practically rescuing them from the misery to which they were subjected due to the lack of opportunities in society.

More than anything, for freeing them from the petty control of the abusive leaders, who only sought their own interest.

All the people in the community came together to help the missionaries build all the houses, so they abandoned collecting garbage since the missionaries gave them food in the time it took them to build the entire community. Thanks to the good relations that he obtained through his merits, and to the recommendations of grandmother, Phillip managed to get some good people interested in a very innovative project, which he had to form to guarantee the progress of the community that they had started, to guarantee a job that would support the cost of a decent life for all families in the community.

Helped by Elida and Raúl, Phillip devised a recycling machine on a scale sufficient to deal with the amount of garbage that was generated from all the communities in the region. Calculating the growth rate of the communities, at Elida's suggestion, and the number of people required for the recycling plant to be functional, by Raúl. That made him feel that every day he was getting closer to that goal of being able to help those poor people who had almost nothing. That is why he did not skimp on details so that everything would be in the best way.

Those who appreciate what you are capable of will support whatever your heart desires. Yours will go with you until the end.

The grandmother met with the state governor to show him the plans to build the recycling plant. She told him about the idea of employing people from the communities of the municipality so that they would have the opportunity to improve their lives with decent and more practical employment.

Thanks to the great respect that the governor had for the grandmother, and in addition to the fact that he realized that it was a magnificent and very innovative project, he agreed very happy to allow the construction of that recycling plant, which he even gave up the land for almost nothing to contribute to the cause. The grandmother told him that the project would be finished just before the new state elections, and that it would be a good example of his part in winning people's votes. She told him that the town needed more governors like him. The governor was delighted with what the grandmother told him, so he promised to contribute state funds to the project so that it would be done as soon as possible, and he promised to give all the permits required for the work.

This marvel of human ingenuity required a master plan to make the process viable, which is why Elida devised a recycling system at home, to facilitate the collection process when it arrived at the plant. She suggested that it was necessary to educate families about the recycling of certain plastic waste, and metals that could be reused, as well as the care of certain toxic waste that could harm people or the environment. It was a project like no other at that time, so many construction companies offered to carry out the construction.

Phillip had very different plans than anyone else might've thought because he sought out Uicho to ask him to take charge of the construction work.

Uicho received them at his house very happy because they had visited him and offered them something to eat and drink at the moment, without knowing what Phillip had prepared for him. He was very surprised when Phillip asked him because he could not believe that he entrusted him with such an obligation. But Chendo reiterated that it was true, in addition to Raúl, who also reiterated it as true. Uicho thanked Phillip, acknowledging the impeccable work he had done, and he was even more grateful that he had chosen him to carry out the construction job. Phillip knew that all his money would be required to guarantee that the job was built according to its purpose, so he spent every penny he had obtained from the sale of his relics, and the little that came out of The Southern Foundation, to that there was no shortage of funds, and so the recycling plant was built in the time he had planned.

With no more funds than his recognitions, he listened attentively to the talks of those two young men who worked in the vineyard with him, and with whom after a while it became a great friendship, and to whom he came to trust with a few personal things; Besides that they really liked to listen to him when he talked about the freedom of the spirit and the good customs that could guide them to their personal fulfillment.

The boys respected him because there was a good spirit in them that made them come closer to Phillip's advice.

On one of those days when he was returning from the day to the mansion, the sunset caught him with its mysterious flashes, which captivated him in a great way, to the point of feeling a great need to meditate for a while.

He stopped between some small trees where only the birds could be heard singing, and the sound of flowing water, which was confused with the wind when it touched the leaves of the trees. He settled as best he could in the middle of the trees, sunbathing his face with that amber light that penetrated his emotions, making him fall into a deep state of meditation, which led him towards a battle where the ego took over his thoughts.

"How is it not to think?" Phillip debated within his personal search.

He gradually got rid of all the noises in his mind, until he reached a state where he found himself in a lonely corner, fearful and confused. His ego did not attack him, so he melted deeper into the moment in that lonely corner.

He felt unconcerned with the external and personal in the world, so he got rid of the body, and traveled at the moment to the pyramid of The Old Lady with the White Hair, who was waiting for him as always sitting on the blue stone.

Nothing surprised him anymore at that moment in his life, since it was not earthly prejudices that worried him when he was in the spirit.

The old lady approached the altar, from where she took one of the many artifacts she had, and pointed it at where

Phillip was, or at the spirit that gave strength to whom they called Phillip, who only looked at her very astonished without knowing what to do, and not quite sure that he understood what the old lady was saying to him.

"Now the key is yours entirely," the old lady told him. "You must continue to your next phase; the spear will wait for you when you are ready."

Phillip was trying to assimilate what was happening when the old lady insisted that he should try to deal more with himself, instead of dealing with or worrying about the problems that the world entertained him with, because that was the true path to the truth, which now it was his turn to protect.

There were no doubts or fears in him at that moment, and no carnal desire or aberration seduced him, so he took everything very seriously, and returned to where his body was when he opened his eyes, at the old lady's request.

Before falling into his silence and escaping from the moment outside his body, in the midst of these trees that were brushed by the wind, a leaf fell from one of the branches, being held by the wind that formed a small whirlpool, which made it fall slowly at the moment when Phillip closed his eyes to meditate. When he opened his eyes, he realized that the leaf of the tree had not yet touched the ground, feeling the impression that he had never left, but his being knew that everything was real, that he had not invented or imagined it.

Some would say that are just hallucinations from the schizophrenia the world experiences, and that the being welcomes with the ideas that are suggested in the model that governs aspirations.

The political and religious media demand an unshakable faith regarding ideas, leaving no room for the opening of conscience, for the freedom of the spirit. Each one judge in your own way. He returned to the mansion standing tall of his convictions, which is why he was very open and helpful to everyone, more than what they were already used to from him. Everyone felt the most comfortable and loved by the happiness that was reflected in his actions and emotions with which he was directed in his service.

The only one who knew something was wrong with him was Elida, who questioned him in their nightly talks, to find out how to support him in what might be happening to him in his conflicting emotions.

"I will always support your decisions. Of course, if your decision is not to tell me, then you have taken me as a stranger." Elida told him as if complaining a little about his silence.

That night they had been talking in the mansion's library to not disturb Moonlight's golden sleep. At the moment Elida said those words to him, Phillip was thinking about the events that were to come, and he did not know precisely what to tell his beloved so that she would not worry about the destiny that the divine had specified in them.

Elida went to the room where Emma was asleep in the cradle and sat by her side to contemplate her while she slept, thinking about those designs that Phillip feared; Well, those that God chooses for his plan are elevated beings that have nothing to do with the prejudices of the material world.

These watchers feel the call within themselves, with the sensation that their spirit has developed, to find themselves on a plane apart from their aching bones and flesh.

That night Elida had a dream, where she felt like she was floating in the air, with her beloved daughter Emma in her arms, and crying very scared. She did not know what was happening, but she had a feeling that it was something that was to come, so she paid close attention to not miss the details in case they were necessary at a given time. The days went by with the same sensation that many of us feel on some occasions when we do not know what we should do,

26

and we wait for something to happen so that our lives change in a certain way, as if a better day were to come, so that our dreams come true. We know that is not so.

Many of us waste our time waiting for life to show us the signs, which we would like to have to know what is the best thing to do, without knowing that it is necessary for each one to seek their destiny in their own way, without waiting for one day everything to change by itself.

On the contrary, seeking destiny is the best way to face the path, to which the spirit must submit to learn the best it can from its own example in carnal life.

They both knew that the best thing they could do was face their destiny without fear of adversities, which they had a presentiment from the signs in their dreams. In addition, Phillip felt that divine protection would be on his side, just as it had been until now. That the purpose was well worth the suffering they had to experience. Although he did not entirely agree, he refused to believe that this was the only way.

The grandmother's lawyers took care of processing a visa so that they could emigrate to that country, which Phillip sensed it would have a great impact on his personal and spiritual life. Just in the time it took them to prepare the necessary things for them to leave, after the first birthday of their beloved daughter Emma.

It was the most awaited date for everyone in the mansion, so they prepared for days preparing all the necessary things to attend to the guests, who were mostly farm workers and their families.

The whole place was filled with flowers everywhere, with all kinds of decorations that people had brought to celebrate Emma's first birthday. Phillip and Chendo made her a special chair, where she would sit to blow out the candles on the cake, which Mama Chayo, Elida, and the cook prepared for two days for the party. Two piñatas were broken that day, with great difficulty by the way, because Elida and the grandmother had made them themselves with the intention that they would last as long as possible, so that the children would have more to entertain themselves before cutting the cake and serving the food. Without a doubt, it was the happiest day that the mansion had had, which reminded everyone of when Elida had her first birthday.

Chapter 2
The Pain of Goodbyes

We always prepare beforehand to celebrate and enjoy the commemorative dates, some of which only last one day. At least almost all the dates that are celebrated around the world, or a few days in some cultures that venerate certain beliefs.

The fervor with which people gather is synonymous with happiness and joy, but sometimes it turns into extremist confusion, due to the ideas that are used to manipulate the interests of a few, who deceive the innocent to act in the interest of these petty untruthful. The same truth that is open to all equally but is twisted to manipulate and deceive. Disinformation for political and religious interests leads to idealistic and existential divisions, which harm equality and the right to freedom.

Those in power will never let us be free of thought or action, in one way or another they twist history to suit their interests, as well as ridicule anyone who tries to warn against their lies.

Now it turns out that what is good is a joke that we should not pay attention to, and what is ridiculous, and irrational is what they suggest we accept as appropriate.

The memory of the good time they had lasted for many days, the joy of the children running all over the garden, and how comfortable people felt with everyone; Well, everyone showed great confidence and satisfaction when being cared for and served by everyone who lived in the mansion. What pleased Elida and Phillip the most was the beautiful sunset in which the universe had shown its gift so that everyone could enjoy that beautiful amber light, which would remain in the memory of many as one of the best sunsets they had ever seen in their lives.

The problem with celebrations is that someone has to clean up after all the mess. No one could deny it.

Even though a few volunteered to help with the cleanup, it took most of the next day for them to get everything back to the way it was before the party.

There is no doubt that teamwork and solidarity is the key to achieving any goal faster and easier. It was because of that feeling of inclusiveness that those of the mansion conveyed with their simplicity and harmony, which is why the workers, and their families enjoyed helping.

People gave Emma endless things that she did not really need but were received with great appreciation and respect. The things that Emma did not use were donated to low-income families, in the first service visit they made to the communities of the region.

One of those days after having returned from giving service to the community, Phillip felt within himself the need to walk through the vineyard to think carefully about what he should do and to be able to guarantee the well-being of those he loved. Thinking about what was best for them, he lost himself in reproaches because of his fears, which tormented him thinking about what could happen in the future with them.

Almost upon reaching the river, he stopped and sat down on the edge of the vineyard, because his stomach began to ache a little from the anguish he felt.

More than anguish, it was the pain he felt when he knew what was to come, because he knew from the visions and premonitions that fate showed him that what he wanted in his heart for those he loved would be something very difficult to achieve, but he also knew that there was a chance that everything would eventually turn out just as the divines had planned, and that made him feel a little better. Enough to be able to enjoy the sunset, which covered Phillip with more melancholy than usual.

Before the sun hid from the night, Gabriel appeared behind the last rays of the amber of the sun just at the moment when Phillip was looking towards the horizon. He approached him with that sublime look on his face, filled with a smile that radiated a contagious light, which no one could contain the seriousness of seeing him. Likewise, Phillip's face filled with a smile that almost came out of his face, when he realized it was him. He hugged him with a great feeling, to the point that tears fell from the emotion of loss and impotence that he could not contain in his chest, asking Gabriel like a disconsolate child the reason for his fate. Gabriel snuggled him against his chest, comforting him, just as a father does with his children anguished by the uncertainty of life and its lessons of pain.

They walked along the riverbank until the moon came out, filling the entire valley with its prevailing light over the night, which showed Phillip a canvas made of life, while he listened to Gabriel's advice, for what fate had in store for him in the coming years.

None of his details referred to material things, or situations that he would have to go through. Rather, he focused on the spiritual and intimate, so that it would not be confused with attachment, according to what Phillip could understand at the time.

"Our father is careful to show us the moment," Gabriel said, pointing to the moon, which had dimmed to a very intense reddish hue. He beholds the mighty wisdom. "Blood Moon" Philip thought.

Gabriel explained that this was the second sign that defined his spirit, in a way that no man had ever achieved, but that not everything was freely given to him, but entrusted to him to carry out the task necessary to achieve a more stable cosmic balance. That he should be aware to not be confused when he has to decide between what is carnal and what is most relevant as a spirit, because there would be moments in which his being would be tested, to ensure that he could achieve sufficient awakening to be able to fight against the tyranny that rule this world.

He gave him precise instructions not to take the medallion or the pectoral with him, on his next migration to that prosperous northern country. That he should focus only on the book for now, and that he should keep what he had entrusted to him in a safe place. Himself suggested that the cave would be the most ideal so that no one could ever become obsessed with The Tools of Order. Well, Phillip was the only one who had the key to gain access.

Phillip noticed Gabriel's insistence, reminding him for the second time to hide the medallion and the pectoral, for which Phillip told him that he had already done it according to his advice, even though he felt he would need them at some point. Phillip did not feel any fear, nor did greed overshadow him, thinking that he had everything to stay in grandmother's mansion because all that was insignificant to him; Well, he was always a beggar who did not participate in the desire to earn money, much less to be famous or popular.

He knew that he should shape his path on his own way, without prejudice leading him to make the mistakes he always avoided but sometimes neglected due to a lack of persistence in paying attention to detail.

He returned to the mansion just as dinner was ready and served on the table, where everyone was reunited as a big family, without prejudice of obligations or class discrimination. No one ate until everyone sat down, and they prayed for the ones in need, in addition to asking God for personal advice for each one, and his guidance to do good at all times. For the first time in many years, they were once again enjoying the warmth of home and true love. Of those unrepeatable moments that on many occasions we tend to ignore, or do not properly value. Phillip watched the happy kids with great pride and happiness, talking as always about things that the older ones try to avoid. His compadre Chendo and Mama Chayo, bathed in laughter talking with their grandmother and Raúl, about their youthful adventures, as if they were great friends.

Phillip remained observing Elida while she gave her beloved daughter Emma something to eat. In the same way, Elida was also observing him at that moment, with that feminine intuition that mothers manage to develop more than fathers. She knew perfectly what was going on in Phillip's mind at that moment, of the great passionate feeling of his life, without prejudices conjuring him to contribute; Well, he was a simple man with no ambition for riches or luxuries, he only longed for wisdom and truth about his spirit, and the vicissitudes that he experiences in carnal life.

Elida interrupted the usual fuss they made every night at dinnertime, asking for everyone's attention, because Phillip had something very important to tell them. Without taking her eyes off her beloved, convinced of his great value as a man and spirit; Well, she already knew all the intimacy of him. She discovered it when she loved him, and by getting lost in the depths of his gaze.

Everyone silenced their laughter of joy and paid attention thanks to the insistence of the youngest of Chendo's sons, who carefully observed what was happening between Elida and Phillip, because it seemed as if they were speaking to each other only with their thoughts. That is why at that moment the boy helped Elida to get everyone's attention, yelling for everyone to be quiet, because Phillip wanted to tell them something. Since they had not listened to Elida very well, because of the laughter that the grandmother and Mama Chayo exaggerated when talking. Phillip explained to them that they should leave, to start their own life as a family, without depending on anyone else. That it was not underestimating the attention the grandmother had given them or for letting them stay in her house for as long as they needed. He did it to also show himself that he was capable of starting from the bottom, like any simple nobleman who tries to earn a living with his abilities, and to be able to build his own legacy.

He wanted to leave an example of nobility and sacrifice for his daughter, so that she would not get used to the comforts she had in the mansion. So that, in some way, she would come to understand a little the intention with his example, but not so that she would think like him, but so that she would consider some vicissitudes, which are necessary to understand the nobility of the spirit, and its tendency to search for the reason of conscience.

He knew perfectly well the risks they had by staying because the masters of lies would look for them no matter where they took refuge, to erase the attempt to bring the truth to light. In addition to the corrupt and greedy misers, that is why he could not afford to risk Elida's stepfather finding out where they were, because sooner or later ambition would tempt him to lose himself even more in his material weakness and try to kill them.

For this and many more personal reasons, Phillip made the decision to migrate to the northern country, because he had better hope of progress and protection for his loved ones.

He knew that this country would play a very important role in his spiritual path, so he felt that he should be in that place to get ready for the moment designated by the divine, in his personal lesson, so that he could awaken to the truth.

The grandmother got up from her chair with a leap of joy and felt a great pride in her chest, because she had remembered the moment when her three children had decided to find their way. She was very happy to know that

34

Phillip had the same ideal as her beloved deceased husband, who tried until the last moments of his life to set an example for his beloved children. The one that gave in his disinterest in serving those most in need.

These three noble children served the people with their lives with all the intentions of their being, thanks to the noble gesture on their father's side. The same one that grew in Phillip's heart, and the same one that Raúl recognized the moment he saw him for the first time.

Raúl got up from the table to congratulate Phillip and give Elida and Emma a hug, because Elida had her in her arms during that time. Raúl kissed each of them on the forehead, with watery eyes knowing that they would go away from them again.

Raúl remembered that day when Elida's mother had made the same decision to face her own destiny, carrying Elida in her arms, in the same chair, and with most of the family together. It seemed as if things were repeated over and over again, so Raúl realizing this, understood the lessons his spirit needed to transcend beyond what the mind can imagine, so he got lost in the singularity of the moment to take advantage of every detail. It seemed to him as if he were in both places at the same time, seeing Josefa carrying Elida, and Elida with Emma in her arms, in the same place and with the same words that Phillip pronounced giving his reasons; Thus, he watched Elida's father say his reasons for starting her own destiny as a family.

The grandmother listened to Phillip very attentively, despite the fact that, for her age, he was just a little boy trying to be brave. She was a very wise woman and open to all opinions, because neither the arrogance nor the apathy confused her when it came to providing care to anyone, regardless of the social status.

The others congratulated them on the great decision they had made, but they showed sad faces knowing that they would walk away from them. Especially Chendo and Mama Chayo, who shed tears because of the great affection they had for them when they felt that they would go away from them. Phillip calmed things down a bit by saying that they would not leave for the rest of their lives, that they should not worry because they would come down every year if possible to visit them, and that they would try to do it especially on Emma's birthday.

The tears dried up a little because of the joy of the children, who kept repeating that they were very proud of Phillip, and immediately they went and hugged him with great affection.

The smallest of the three said, "I know we'll see each other again." At that moment everyone laughed at the sympathy with which the child had said those words.

After dinner, and having put the children to bed, they met in the mansion's library to discuss the details of how and when their departure would be. Each one gave their opinion trying to persuade them that the best decision was to stay in the mansion, since they had no need to emigrate anywhere, because they would not find the comfort or affection that they were willing to give them anywhere.

Neither Elida nor Phillip doubted that this was true, but as he had already told them, he wanted to live his life his way, so he asked for their support and understanding.

No one could deny Phillip's words, so very sadly they accepted the idea that the decision had been made, that there would be no turning back for any reason. In addition to the fact that they themselves recognized the dangers they possibly had by staying, because sooner or later the wicked would manage to locate them. The only thing left for them to do was support them in whatever way they could, which they did without hesitation.

The grandmother, thanks to her confidence and friendship with the state governor, had obtained the visas so that they could travel without any problem. The governor had good relations with the embassy of that country, and it was not difficult for him to get the visas without any setbacks.

They were all somewhat sad because they would leave very soon, according to the plans that they all agreed on that night, about what they should do depending on the situations that arose at a certain time.

Either because Elida's stepfather tried to follow them to kill them, or that those illuminated by lies located them to annihilate them all. That was something that they all agreed to very responsibly, in each of their tasks to be done so that they could never be located.

Everyone in the mansion knew perfectly well the risks they were running, after what they had experienced so far, so they did not skimp on details to make sure they would agree to everything that could possibly happen.

Those days of farewell hurt everyone because they felt that they were going to be missed, even before they left, because they really loved them. The only good thing they could give them was their advice, that is why no one missed the moment to talk with them about the unexpected things that could occur in life, so they should be careful when making any decision.

One and a thousand sets of advice each suggested that more than advice they were wishes of the soul so that nothing would happen to them, which Elida and Phillip understood perfectly, so none of them took it lightly.

The grandmother imposed the custom of gathering all the women of the mansion in the garden that her husband had built, so that their three children could enjoy their stay and serve as inspiration in their lives. At that place they enjoyed their last days together, and they tried to make every second last forever, despite the fact that it really seemed as if time passed three times faster, that sometimes they even stayed up very late refusing to accept that it was time for dinner.

Mama Chayo helped her knit a lot of little jackets for little Emma because her grandmother had told them that it was very cold in some of the places they wanted to emigrate to. That is why all the women helped each other to create a dress worthy of a princess for her. Not only for winter, because they also made some clothes for her so that she could wear them in each season of the year.

Elida did not refuse the advice of her loved ones, knowing that they did it with all their hearts, because she felt the melancholy of the farewell in the same way.

On many occasions she had to hold back the urge to cry when she saw them very passionately weaving with much love those beautiful dresses for Moonlight.

On some occasions their feelings overcame, so they cried in each other's arms as the sun went down, and promised each other that they would always be willing to help each other in any way possible. Without hesitation, they reiterated how much they loved each other, and how willing they were to give their lives for any of them.

They all gathered around Emma holding hands to sing to her the songs that Elida's mother sang to her when she was a child, just before the sun went down, on those flushed sunsets with which the universe testified its love.

Each one packed the essentials in their suitcases, just a few objects of personal importance, and five changes of clothes, in addition to a cap that Phillip liked very much, which was very characteristic during that time.

The grandmother gave Elida a hat made by a designer named Vuitton, which her husband had given her when they had completed their first year of marriage. Elida was very happy to know that it would finally be hers, that hat that she admired since she was a child. She remembered those days when grandmother would wear it to go for a walk with grandpa.

"Merci beaucoup, grand mère," Elida told her.

38

"I would give my soul to see you all happy, my little cocoon of love. Your grandfather gave it to me one beautiful afternoon in Paris. Besides that, he made me promise to give it to our first granddaughter. Can you imagine such a thing? We still hadn't planned on the children, and this beau was proposing grandchildren. That's why I fell in love with him, because of his great vision of things, but above all his vision in life." She paused and sighed. "How much I have missed him."

Elida, touched by the feeling of seeing her grandmother remembering her grandfather with so much love, she got up immediately to hug her and gave her a big kiss on the cheek, telling her that she loved her. The grandmother gave her a kiss on her forehead while her tears fell down Elida's face, at the moment that she told her that she loved them in the same way.

The sunlight came in through the window, bathing little Emma with a great luminosity, who by the white sheets seemed to shine by herself. The moment Elida got up from the chair, the hat fell on Emma's head, just at the moment when she tried to put it on top of the stroller where Moonlight was. The hat slipped off thanks to a breeze of air that blew hard enough to land right on her head.

Phillip had time to say goodbye to his new friends, who worked with him in the vineyard, and to talk for a while with that boy who had told him about his cousin's adventure when he crossed the border. For some strange reason, he wanted to know about some details that could be of use to him one day; well, he had a presentiment that his destiny would lead him at some point to the same circumstances that the daring emigrant had experienced. His lifelong great friend accompanied him at all times, as it was common for both of them, but this time it was more significant because he would be leaving them very soon. Chendo took the time to express everything he felt for his great friend, that more than just a friend he loved him like a brother. That was why he felt very sad.

"I won't be gone forever, Bubba," Phillip told him, seeing him very sentimental about the subject.

With a few days to go before they left, Raúl and Phillip took a walk through the vineyard, right next to the river where Phillip liked to go in the afternoons to meditate. They talked about some issues that worried Phillip because he wanted to make sure that Elida's stepfather would never find out about their whereabouts. He made Raúl promise about some things that he should do at a certain moment, which were not clear to him at that moment, but that in its due time he would tell him what it was about.

Raúl trusted Phillip because of the great character of spirit that he reflected, because he reminded him of his great soul friend in those famous days of youth, for this reason he promised to carry out everything he asked of him, after having listened to some of the reasons that Phillip sensed. Since he knew him very well, he did not doubt the advice that Phillip gave him, despite being much older than him. Raúl had recognized the wisdom that Phillip professed with his words, with his advices of an old man; being still very young. That was what caught his attention, and he recognized firmly in his heart that Philip was destined by God to do something extraordinary, but he was not sure what it was. That was what convinced him to take what Phillip was suggesting seriously.

Phillip gave him precise instructions on how and where he would communicate with him, so that there would be no trace that the villains could take advantage of to discover their whereabouts. That he should not take anyone else with him at any time, because only then he would prevent any mortal from knowing the communication channel they would use.

Raúl was somewhat skeptical of the medium that he had suggested because it seemed to him not very realistic that we say. Phillip had asked him to visit The Old Lady with the

White Hair, to be able to communicate with him, because she would give him all the necessary instructions on how and when he could visit her to receive his messages if necessary. "Trust me" Phillip told him, while he placed his hand on Raúl's chest, who smiled at him a bit incredulous, but then accepted willingly seeing Phillip's decision in his eyes. He could not find the trace left by the lie, nor the uncertainty in his words, since Phillip was most secure and firm in his convictions because at that moment he already had the certainty of his destiny, he just needed to see for himself how it was that events would unfold, which would take him to the right place and time to be able to test his intention to help without expecting something in return.

Phillip knew that nothing in life was certain, only carnal death was guaranteed, but the moment and the way would change according to our decisions, those that could influence the event.

He knew that everything could change at any moment, no matter what he sensed and saw in his visions and dreams. He realized that on a few occasions, where he would test himself to experiment on what would happen if he intervened or not in some of his visions.

This is how Phillip realized the freedom of the spirit in the carnal life, and that it was only in this life that such a task could be carried out, which was necessary for the spiritual growth of each being.

Phillip entrusted some special things to Raúl, so that he would not feel alien to the divine mandates, so he would know that he was part of everything that happened; Well, at the right time he will receive the impulse generated by the spirit of goodness, so that he can carry out his task of learning by helping others.

He asked him to take him to the town where they had built his architectural design, because he wanted to take some things for the poor in that town, before going abroad. Raúl did not hesitate to do everything Phillip suggested, so very happy next to Chendo he prepared the truck so that everyone could go with them.

He took the time to live as much as possible with everyone at all times, even on the way to town he enjoyed the innocent talks of the children, who wisely filled the doubts of the elderly, without that being their intention. Or perhaps, that was the intention of the spirits that guide us in our lives, and they used the nobility of the little ones to transmit their advice.

Mama Chayo was never separated from Elida, advising her, and telling her many things that she had not been able to share with her. The truth was that she was not resigned to the idea that they would leave her side very soon, and she did not know how or when she would see them again; Well, she had come to love her as if she were her daughter, and it tore her soul in two to know that she would walk away from her.

Elida's grandmother had realized the affection that Mama Chayo had placed in her granddaughter, and she loved Emma as if she were her own grandmother, that is why she recognized that poor woman with a higher spirit, as if she were part of her family.

The grandmother knew that Elida would have to face her own path in her own way, just as they wanted to try abroad, so she supported the idea, despite knowing the dangers they ran.

Phillip took it upon himself to tell her everything that had happened in the town chapel where Father Joaquín preached, about some things that happened when they lived in the dump, that is why the grandmother helped them leave as safely as possible, but without so much fuss to not raise gossip that could reach the ears of the evil liars.

They brought food for the children of the parish school, as well as clothes and shoes, which Raúl was in charge of getting from some of his acquaintances in the state capital.

The grandmother, Mama Chayo and Elida were in charge of giving personal hygiene products to the mothers of the children, as well as talks about care and remedies to counteract infections at home, as well as the importance of mutual respect. Which, due to the feeling of the spirit towards the good, we know that it must be promoted at home first, with good education of respect for life, with the common sense of goodness and honesty.

Phillip took advantage of a moment of respite to take Raúl to the old lady's house and show him the place, but he had to ask him to walk so that no one could follow them, in case they were spying on them.

They even had to change their clothes to be sure that no one would recognize them, so they wore the old clothes that Phillip kept in one of his trunks, just for that occasion, according to him.

On the way Phillip took the opportunity to show Raúl some houses where he had been kicked out for looking unpleasant when he lived in the dump and walked the streets.

Raúl recognized some of the houses among which they had received help from the foundations that Phillip had made, and he was greatly surprised to learn how the people had treated him, and even so, Phillip had helped them. Immediately recognizing the great heart that God had given Phillip, he hugged him with his face full of tears because of the great feeling he felt in his chest and told him that he was very proud of him, by the grace of the goodness of him. They continued walking to a house where a leafy laurel grew, to get some shade, because the sun was hitting very hard at that time of day.

Raúl listened to the wisdom that Phillip transmitted to him about his experiences, with great respect and attention, since he recognized the strength and wisdom of Phillip's spirit.

As they were talking about some vicissitudes, a lady came out yelling at them to get out of that place, because they stunk and looked bad, throwing water at them to make them move.

"Fuck off here you fucking stinking filthy!" The lady shouted, "I don't know why I can't stand these people, that makes me feel I don't know how!"

Phillip pulled Raúl by the arm to save him from burning himself with the hot water that the lady had thrown at them, in her outburst of hatred for their insecurities and weaknesses.

Raúl had remained motionless looking at the lady who was approaching them without hesitating, with her face full of disgust and revulsion, which caused him a nervous breakdown when he saw that the lady had dared to throw the hot water at them.

He could not believe that scene that was taking place before him, because it was difficult for him to recognize the truth from his own experience, and he could not contain his tears in the middle of the street.

As soon as he managed to avoid the hatred of the poor woman, ignorant of her own condition, he fell to his knees with a great pain in his heart, because he remembered that himself had been the one who had delivered to that family the goods that Phillip had designated for them. Phillip took his arm to help him get up, trying to explain what was happening with a different meaning than ego or vanity; Well, he tried to tell him that it was not about anyone else, it was just about himself, before judging the imperfection in others; Well, if it is possible to differentiate between what is done, it is possible to understand the actions that others do before us, not to judge them, but to learn.

"Tell me, Raúl... what did you learn from this?" Phillip asked him, when Raúl was gaining some strength, and he recognized the lesson that life was giving him.

The lady had not recognized him because of the beggar's clothing that Phillip lent him for the occasion, even though she had received the money from Raúl. But it had been a different situation where Raúl dressed very differently from how he was that day with Phillip in The Street of Bitterness. Each one judge in your own way.

With enough lucidity he followed Phillip for a few more blocks, listening to his teachings with the same amusement that a child has when learning something new.

Phillip told him the fable of the marbles and their symbolism in the modern world, about the plot that rulers invent to dominate over the innocent. Raúl tried to understand that parable, understanding firsthand the injustice and inequality that is experienced everywhere. In addition to all the lies that the powerful use to dominate and deceive the world population.

He recognized how right Philip was in referring to those ill-intentioned as petty puppeteers.

With his back to the old lady's house, looking towards the adobe wall where the children were playing marbles, Phillip recognized in Raúl the intention that the divine leave in their chosen ones, and told him that he was ready to take his next step in his spiritual life.

He took him by the shoulder with his right hand, pointing with his left hand towards the old lady's house, as a kind invitation to continue.

"Come on, she's surely waiting for us." Philip told him.

At the entrance to the house, Raúl felt a little dizzy from the confusion that was going through his mind, because at that moment he heard the old lady's words in his head. He did not know what to do, even he fainted a little from shock. Phillip helped him, telling him not to be afraid, that he would soon know the reason for what was happening to him, not to worry, and that he should continue without hesitation.

He took his arm to help him up, not intending to pressure him to continue; Also, he told him that it was his personal decision, that if he wanted, they would leave that place at the time he required it, but if he wanted to continue, he should face his fears before taking the next step in his personal reunion.

Raúl was old and very wise, but not as much. He took courage in his faith and walked by Phillip's side to where the old lady was sitting on the blue stone waiting for them.

The Old Lady with the White Hair looked at them with great complacency when they were in front of her. So Raúl felt safe, but still a bit disconcerted for having heard the old lady tell him that she was waiting for him. He kept looking into her eyes, surprised to be able to listen to her without saying a single word with her mouth, with his eyes that almost bulged out of his face.

He had to face all his beliefs before accepting that all this was happening because there was a moment in which he doubted that all this was true. He consciously accepted and now convinced that everything was possible, so he felt brave enough to continue as far as he had to go. He was willing.

Phillip stayed by his side, watching what was happening, because he knew from his own experience that all this was necessary for Raúl to face his fears and discover the true path of the spirit in carnal life.

The old lady got down from the blue stone and walked towards Raúl with the spear in her right hand, she put it in Raúl's chest, which caused him to cough.

In an instant, for reasons that only happened inside his head, he began to cry with great feeling, repeating to himself: "I didn't know, I didn't know." Raúl recognized in his heart the mistakes that he had made in his life and accepted the naivety with which he unintentionally hurt others, for which he regretted everything that he could have caused to the innocent with his words or facts.

With the spirits on the ground, bathed in tears of repentance, he stood up trying to wipe away his tears with his hands. The old lady smiled when she saw that Raúl's heart became different from the heart with which the world loses itself in pleasures, and she gave him a drink from a bowl that would calm him down for the moment.

Raúl took the bowl still whimpering a little because of what he felt, because he had some visions at the moment the old lady pointed the spear at him, which made him see how cruel we can become with our fellow men, with the acts that we consider suitable for us, but for them it turns into lost dreams, and without hope for their desires or needs.

Taking the first sip, he realized that it was very sweet on the palate, but bitter in his belly, so he began to squirm in anguish as he remembered the pain his indifference had caused. He ended up lying on the ground, without Phillip or the old lady intervening, since it had to do with his own being, the pain caused by the ingratitude of our pride and the voracity of our ego. After a few minutes, he calmed down a bit, because the pain disappeared as he repented of his mistakes. He felt a different awareness from how he commonly judged what he understood of reality, continuing for a few minutes to fight with the thoughts that the ego counteracted in his new vision of life.

"The scourge of the world, and accomplice of vanity. Don't let it poison your heart or confuse your spirit." The old lady told Raúl, while he was staring into her eyes, because he had noticed a white light that radiated from her head, which even came out of her eyes, ears, and through her mouth when speaking.

All this was new to him, but he was determined to continue until he found the reason why he had come to this world, and discover the truth for his own being, about the destiny of his existence after the carnal life.

After chatting with Raúl for a few minutes about precise instructions on what he should do to find his balance in energy, and what he should eat to achieve an adequate state of health to energize these key points in the body, the old lady gave him on a piece of paper a special herbal recipe that should be mixed with other necessary elements for the potion to take effect.

The old lady spoke with Phillip about what he should do at a certain moment because he should be persistent in his intentions so that he would not fail when deciding what is right for his purpose. Phillip promised to be prudent and sincere when accepting the responsibilities that corresponded to him, but he did not guarantee that everything would be perfect since he was not perfect, that it would be logical if he failed in something. The old lady just looked at him and smiled knowing that Phillip was right.

Even though, she reminded him how important it was to try to do his best, because only then could the goal be achieved. Phillip accepted and promised to do everything in his power to achieve it.

In the same way, Raúl took his new responsibilities very seriously, despite not yet fully understanding his purpose as a spirit. He promised to be patient and prudent with all that was entrusted to him, and he promised to learn everything that was necessary to be prepared. Now he felt that everything was different, starting with himself, because he could no longer deny that part of the truth that had been revealed within his being.

In the end they decided to return to the village parish to meet the others, and to be able to return to the mansion before nightfall, since it would take them a few hours to return to the region where they lived with the grandmother.

That was his last charity visit in that town, which had taught him a bit of his personal lesson, with the friction of his experiences with the beings that formed his criteria and his feeling towards reality.

Phillip was grateful for the compliments and insults that people gave him, according to his moment and his purpose. That was how Phillip perceived him, due to the melancholy that goodbyes cause. I do not know if that happens with everyone.

In the mansion, the sad faces increased as the day they would leave drew closer and closer, because it was something that nobody wanted to happen. But they knew it was necessary in order to save Moonlight's innocent life from the clutches of liars, and their own as well.

That day nobody wanted to come, they got up earlier than usual to prepare everything they needed for their trip. Not just Phillip and Elida, because they were all in the living room waiting for them to come out of their room, and to be able to enjoy their company for a few hours before they left at noon. It was certainly the fastest hours everyone has ever experienced in their lives, not wanting time to pass by not even a second.

Inevitably everyone resigned themselves to letting them go, even though they did not accept or approve of it in any way, so it became a dark day filled with sorrow for their departure.

They only took three suitcases, so that they could move without much effort when they had to change the bus, as planned by Raúl and Phillip.

A small bag that Elida used to store things that Emma might need on the way, and the backpack that Phillip used all the time, where he kept the most basic things to keep himself sane about who he was and where he came from.

Raúl took them on The Great Eagle to the state capital, where they would take their first travel bus, which would take them to the country's border. The grandmother accompanied them until they boarded the bus, as did Raúl, who helped Phillip load the suitcases into the bus compartment. He gave him a hug of thanks for all that he had taught and advised; because, even for an old man of more than sixty years, he took very seriously the role that Phillip had before the divine and respected his wisdom. The grandmother said goodbye to

Elida and Emma with tears on her face, heartbroken and inconsolable, hugging them until the moment when Phillip had to insist that the bus was about to leave. The grandmother hugged him in the same way, asking him to be brave, and that he would never let anyone hurt them ever. Phillip promised to give his life so that everything would be different, no matter what.

They boarded the bus at six in the evening, in time to enjoy the beautiful sunset.

Chapter 3
The Epiphany Of Regret

That one who has had to leave their place of origin, knows the melancholy of goodbyes, and hopes for the future. How the road becomes difficult due to the sadness of thinking about the loved ones we leave behind, without knowing if we will see them again one day. It is difficult to get rid of the loving attachment to other beings that make us happy, of their smiles and their anger.

Elida still carried the pain of losing her mother, and she sort of never got over the death of her father. She always thought of the absence that he made during all those years of pain that she lived without his advice, without his affection. Deep inside her, she knew that at some point in her existence, she would see them again, and she took comfort in the idea of her accepting that death was natural for everyone; Well, it does not discriminate against any organic being on this planet, which dies and is resurrected in each one of us.

She clung to Moonlight against her chest, to protect her from the cold that it was at that time of year, almost at the exact moment when Phillip hugged them and told them how much he loved them. As an inevitable indication of what fate had prepared for them on that confusing and uncertain path of life.

Sheltered between his chest, Elida wondered why the innocent always lost and the wicked liars triumphed. She was undoubtedly a long way from finding the answer that would excuse such, although she did not believe that there was any excuse for evil. In any case, she tried not to lightly judge what she did not know about the divines and their mysterious plan for the spirit, so to not fall into the ignorance that blinds the awakening of consciousness.

The trip from the state capital to the northern neighboring state, of just nine hours away, turned somewhat funny when a couple of clowns, who were traveling to the capital city of that state, let their instincts of happiness flow for a few hours of travel, making it seem like only a few hours, for the sympathy and charisma with which their souls boasted of their happiness, which characterizes those who try to cause a healthy smile in our world.

Unfortunately, many underestimate those humble details with which the appropriate ones express themselves, to give us a moment of detachment from daily concerns, missing out on the opportunity to discover for themselves the key to freeing themselves from doubt or pain for not understanding happiness. Pain is indeed part of the lesson, but that doesn't mean that we should feed it while suffering with the inability to let it go. We must let it flow to be able to realize the difference between laughter and crying, between bitterness and the joy of seeing the light.

Detachment is important and necessary, especially detaching of what doesn't let us live or think freely. Believing is deceptive, freedom is thinking that everything is possible, that God is all possibility, without limit.

Two ladies and an old woman were traveling in the front seat. A nine-year-old boy and a three-year-old girl were traveling in the seat parallel to them.

For a few hours of the trip, the girl spent her time asking Elida about Emma and what they gave her to eat, along with a thousand more questions about how and when she was born. In a mannered way, Elida responded to that innocent girl every question that disturbed her, because of the good feeling that her chest has when recognizing good beings, well she felt that that girl was a very elevated being, who appeared on their way to protect them. So, it was necessary to listen

52

carefully at the right time. Nothing surprised her anymore; she did not limit herself to thinking that everything was possible. With the love and attention that only a mother gives her children, she listened with a free mind and an open heart to that little girl, who kept asking her endless questions about Moonlight.

Phillip, with his mind overflowing with thoughts that tormented him about what could happen in the near future with his family, did not realize the details that the girl discussed with Elida, which he would understand long after that melancholic and sad afternoon., in which they had to flee to save the life of an innocent being, who would take her time to grow up before claiming her throne, with the example of the nobility for serving and giving without expecting anything in return. It goes without saying that Emma's spiritual nature was alien to the interests of the greedy and corrupt. Those who insist on deceiving all weak-minded, all those who have a confused and ill-cared heart, to carry out their plans of control and submission, which rule in this world full of lies and indifference.

I believe that everyone has their own personal lesson in life, and no one could tell you what you had to do at a certain point in your life. Perhaps, if advice is suggested to us by other spirits on some occasions, we could understand the difference regarding the correct thing to do in a given circumstance; and that is why we must consider the experiences of those who try to advise us about something in our lives.

I understand that it can be difficult for some to understand that the spirits can advise us, and for others it is mostly natural in their faith. Do not forget that the living are also spirits, who advise us with their disinterested intention, so that we grow a little more in our path as spiritual beings.

Something that is very true in this life is that we are not alone in the infinite universe of our creator, because we are the very creation of his intentions, the primordial purpose, his personal epiphany. It is in ourselves, the way in which the universe consciously recognizes itself, experiencing the infinite range of vicissitudes and sensations in each one of us. Each one judge in your own way.

In some towns the bus stopped so passengers could buy something to eat, relieve themselves, or simply get some fresh air.

In one of those towns, Phillip went down first to get them something to eat just in case something happened at some point. He was no longer blinded to anything that could happen to him, knowing what the greedy and corrupt wretches were capable of doing.

Elida spent a little time wrapping Moonlight up to protect her from the night breeze, and then she went down and stayed a few meters from the bus door, waiting for Phillip to come back so he could take care of Emma for a while, so she could go use the restroom at the truck station.

In fact, Phillip returned as soon as he could and took care of Emma during the time that Elida returned from the restroom. We must remember that it is the obligation of both take care of their offspring, their bud of love. Mutual support is one of the most important things as a couple.

Elida returned just in time for the driver to board the bus, saying that it was time to leave, that he would not stop for anyone.

They boarded the bus quickly, almost running after the driver, just before he closed the door. Phillip immediately tried to protect his loved ones from being hurt by the aggressiveness with which the driver had tried to close the door, which caught the heel of Phillip's right foot, which prevented the door from closing completely, preventing it from crushing Emma's hand that was sticking out from between Elida's arms. Just at the moment when Phillip almost had to push them because of the ingratitude with which the driver had judged them.

The ladies who were sitting next to them got up immediately to help Elida up the stairs to the bus entrance, while Phillip tried to free the heel stuck in the door, because the driver did not deign to open it a bit so that it would be released; rather, he ignored it, and he did not even deign to turn to see him.

Phillip freed himself from the door as best as he could, a little annoyed with the driver for what he had provoked, immediately complaining about his arbitrariness and detachment.

At the same time, he felt that he was making a mistake in trying to complain about his ignorance, so at that moment he stopped blaming the driver, and instead went to help his beloved to get comfortable in the seat, because the unfortunate ungrateful started the truck at the exact moment when Elida had managed to sit down.

One of the ladies fell to the ground due to the sudden outburst with which the driver was trying to release his frustration, but at that moment Phillip launched himself and managed to prevent the lady from hitting her head, almost literally saving her life.

Each one grabbed their seats as best they could because the driver took off as if the devil was chasing him. Many passengers complained almost yelling at him to watch what he was doing, but he paid no attention to their claims, his pride triumphed over everything and everyone.

Leaving the town, the driver gained some lucidity and somewhat slowed down the anger with which he was lost in his thoughts, which made him recognize his mistake in trying to get even with others, for the pain that the pressures caused him, crying out like a heartbroken child. "Nobody knows what's happening to me... Excuse me, I don't know what happened to me," said the driver, trying to wipe his tears with the sleeve of his coat, still whimpering from the epiphany that his thoughts had taught him, upon recognizing the mistake he had made, and at the same time accepting the guilt, which was dissolved by the repentance in his heart. That was something that nobody expected, besides that nobody cared because his grotesque and rude reaction had hurt the little trust they had in him.

Phillip was watching him from his seat, with his hand inside his backpack touching The Book of Raziel, at the moment the driver recognized his mistake. Phillip understood what was happening to that poor man, and he knew that he would need the right advice to continue with the intention indefinitely, despite the difficulties that might arise.

Most of them were still very angry with the driver for the way he had behaved with everyone, so they did not care much to see him cry, they were even reluctant to show any gesture of compassion for that poor man, who was just trying to understand his part in life.

"Poor man, he didn't know, mom" said the youngest of the ladies.

Her mother nodded her head, and hugged her, rubbing her shoulder, which had been hurt when she fell to the ground. The other lady joined them in a big huddle, and with tears on her face to see that man repent with all his heart, in the middle of the road and driving a bus with fourteen passengers.

Knowing that the man needed his advice, Phillip stood up and walked to the seat behind the driver and sat down without saying a single word. The driver had noticed because he saw it in the rearview mirror at the moment he was sitting in the back seat.

There was a moment when they looked at each other, just long enough for the driver to realize the intention of kindness with which Phillip approached him, despite the fact that he had hurt his heel with the door, and that almost hurt his family. Shame lit his face with that unmistakable grimace, so he cried when he recognized what he had done in that fit of stupidity, for not understanding his part in life, and trying to take it out on others for the frustration he felt at that moment. It is a pity that many have to suffer from the ignorance with which ingratitude often confuses us, when we take it out on the innocent for the pain caused by feeling misunderstood.

The driver, named Macedonio Ceniceros Moreno, did not know whether to stop or continue driving the bus, due to the avalanche of emotions he felt, and the grief that overwhelmed him.

The idea of stopping or at least slowing down a bit to not put anyone's life at risk crossed his mind, because the ingratitude he had committed was already enough, and he did not want anything else to happen being his fault.

As he slowed down, he felt a little more confident and able to drive safely, so he decided not to stop the bus, because they were already a little late and he did not want to get scolded again.

He had arrived somewhat late at the town where they had stopped, for which the inspector had strongly scolded him for being late. Reproaching him that it was not the first time he did it, but that if he continued like that it would be the last time he would do it. This being the drop that had spilled the glass in the Macedonian conflicts, which made him explode with fury when he saw that his arguments were not heard. Despite the fact that he tried in many ways to explain to the inspector the details that had occurred on the trip so he should understand that sometimes they happened, and nothing could be done to avoid them.

The inspector was inflexible in his accusations, not listening to what Macedonio had to say in his favor, because he was also under pressure from the regional coordinator, regarding the punctuality of the transport service in that region, since some cases had been reported of delays. The inspector reproached him for the demands of his boss, blaming him for the delays, and was emphatic with his decision to fire him if he were to be late again.

At that moment, he demanded that he leave immediately so that he could reach his next destination on time, threatening to reduce his commissions if he did not do so at that time. That had been the reason why Macedonio had stormed out of the inspector's office.

"I understand you, and I'm not trying to judge you." Philip told him.

The driver narrated to him every vestige that the past had kept inside of him, from the death of his mother, the disappearance of his father, and the murder of his three sisters. His marriage had failed in the same way as his two previous ones, due to infidelity, because he spent more time on the road than in his house. That was why his wife had to find a substitute in her bed.

Loneliness and lack of love incite our needs for affection, and make us vulnerable to any hope, which we pursue with the intention of alleviating a little pain or loneliness, without realizing that we were wrong.

It is necessary that we live in our own flesh the vicissitudes that life has for each of us, to learn from these lessons, which the creator tends on our steps in carnal life. The interesting thing about all this is that, although it seems that we all experience similar things, each one of us has a specific and unique lesson when it comes to facing life, although they are also similar in the nature of human life in particular, not being so different from each other. The message is spiritual, but let us remember that we are all spirits, so the lesson does have some similarity at the end of it. It is necessary for each one to discover your own message and your responsibility as a spirit.

Here is a key for anyone who is interested in discovering one of the best ways to transcend a little on that path that the spirit experiences in carnal life, taking advantage of the advice that often bothers us when confronting our ego and vanity. We know very well that no matter how much advice you give to the young, many will not listen to the experiences of the old.

After a while, the lady who had fallen to the ground when the driver had taken off without any consideration went and sat next to Phillip to tell the driver not to worry, that these things happen all the time, but what had happened afterwards was not something very common in men. That he should feel very happy and proud for having accepted the blame for his actions.

After several hours of healthy conversation between the three of them, an atmosphere of trust was created that helped Macedonio to better understand his condition in life; In addition, he became seriously interested in the subject that Phillip was trying to communicate to him, so that he would seek for himself the answers that were troubling him.

The lady named Socorro Ceniceros, explained to Macedonio about the root of ego and vanity, and how to counteract attachment to what does not make us free as spiritual beings. Phillip looked at her in a way, as if trying to understand a little how it was that the lady knew everything that he felt, so to not lose any detail in case he was asleep dreaming about what he was experiencing, which made him think seriously about reality and the visions he had.

He was able to differentiate after a long time of introspection that he was awake, but he tried to remember if he'd had any vision regarding what was happening, or what was about to happen.

The peculiarity of the moment distracted him a little from his attempt to remember the detail, which would warn him about an important event on his way, but he did not specify the moment or the detail. He felt that he had already lived that moment, and he tried to specify what was to come. The other lady had sat in Phillip's place, next to Elida to talk and make the trip more enjoyable. The lady's mother joined the conversation, as did the two children. Especially the little girl, who kept asking and asking about the way they took care of Moonlight.

"Excuse her, since she was born my daughter has been very weird," the lady said to Elida. "She is the same as my sister Socorro."

"Look, I've already understood it well myself," Elida replied, referring to Phillip.

At that moment, upon hearing Elida say those words, Phillip was able to remember the vision of what was about to happen, and asked the driver to stop immediately, and that he should trust him if he wanted to continue living. Socorro replied to the driver to do what Phillip was asking, for which the driver became very nervous, not knowing what to do.

"The poet is right, Macedonio. Stop it now," Socorro told the driver.

Phillip turned to see Elida and she nodded her head as a sign that Phillip was right. He knew that he should warn others about what was about to happen, so that they would try to save their lives from the clutches of corrupt misers who deceive the innocent. He hesitated a bit, thinking that they would only judge him for being crazy, not knowing how to clarify or explain to them what they were about to face. In any case, he dared to know that maybe they would not care, since his only intention was to try to save their lives, regardless of their ignorance or their vanity.

Some were asleep and did not hear what Phillip was yelling at them, despite the fact that he moved them a little with his hand to make them react. The children hugged Elida along with the ladies, as if protecting Emma.

Phillip called Macedonio by name to stop the bus, who stopped immediately, at the moment when Phillip ran to open the back door so they could escape. Some passengers complained about what was happening, and asked the driver not to stop, to ignore that crazy man. Macedonio did everything as Phillip asked him to, regardless of what the people were demanding of him; he even knew that he could lose his job.

Phillip got off first to help Elida and Emma, then he helped Macedonio get the children and ladies off the bus. Once down, all those who chose to follow them, he asked them to immediately run towards a pile of rocks that protruded from the ground, which were also covered by greasewood. Phillip led the way, while Macedonio stayed behind the children and the ladies to take care of their backs.

While they ran towards the stones, Phillip gave them instructions on what they had to do when he tells them, so they would not be discovered.

One of the passengers yelled at them that they were crazy, but Phillip insisted that they ignore him and pay no attention to fools.

Almost upon reaching the stones, Macedonio turned to see the man who misjudged them, and tripped over a stone for not looking where he was going, so he fell to the ground hitting his heel. Phillip helped him up as soon as possible, asking him not to look back.

Macedonio was seduced by curiosity to see what was going to happen, turning to see once more.

Curiosity and doubt always bring us trouble. I do not know if it is due to the lack of faith, or the fear that we cannot contain.

He could not believe what was happening before his eyes, which terrified him because he could see how the bus looked like it was still running on the road, and that someone was driving it. He fainted a little when he saw that the driver who was driving the bus was himself. So, he fell into a state of nervousness from the shock of seeing what was happening, which had nothing to do with what was supposed to happen.

Phillip had to carry him so they could hide in time, just at the moment when two trucks with armed men stopped the bus. Asked them not to make any noise, whatever happened, not to be afraid, but to cover the children's ears.

Macedonio, with a frightened face, with eyes that almost bulged out of his face, hugged the child, and covered his ears. Socorro covered the girl's ears, and she stared into her eyes; for which, the girl only nodded her head, as if she heard what Socorro was trying to say.

At that moment, Phillip realized that he was not the only one who was on this path that the divine prepare to teach us the way to carry out their plans, when contemplating the inheritance of the gifts that are imparted among the spirits, in the action that Socorro practiced with the girl.

Elida covered Emma's ears so she would not be scared, while Phillip covered her ears, and she stared into his eyes. He was able to realize that Moonlight was staring into his eyes, then little Emma nodded her head, at the moment that he told her with the thought that everything would be fine.

The gunmen took all the passengers off the bus and murdered them in cold blood, after asking each one by name.

Phillip and Macedonio listened when the head of the armed commando asked his deputy to make sure he killed everyone, after checking their names on the passenger list, and when he was done, he would bring the list to him.

The tyrant's truck had been left near the rocks where they were hiding, so they could hear clearly when he called his boss on the shortwave radio, telling him that the job was done, that they had already killed them all.

Macedonio, with a scared face and his heart about to beat out of his chest, stared into Phillip's eyes, trying to find a reason for what was happening, while Phillip only grimaced telling him to trust him. Macedonio turned to Socorro, who nodded her head as a sign that he should do what Phillip was suggesting. The other Lady and her mother covered each

62

other's ears and kept their eyes closed. In a few minutes the criminals disappeared in the same way as they had arrived, leaving no trace of where they had come from or where they had gone.

Phillip reacted immediately, asking Macedonio to accompany him, to retrieve some suitcases that were essential for little Emma; Therefore, Macedonio did not feel very encouraged to want to help him, because he was still very confused by what had happened.

Socorro asked him to help him, that she would take care of the others, that he also had the key to the trunk. That he should not be afraid that he could trust them because they were the good ones. Macedonio accepted almost scared to death, so Phillip insisted that he should trust him. That they would have to act immediately to get out of that place, because there was a possibility that the criminals would return.

They got close enough to see the bodies next to the truck, but Macedonio could not see any bodies anywhere, nor any blood.

The bus was intact, stopped in the middle of the road, with only the back door open, just as he had left it when he got off. Phillip asked him not to look, to fight his curiosity and concentrate solely on what they had to do.

"This is witchcraft," Macedonio murmured at that moment.

"Macedonio, trust me," Phillip told him, "we are the good ones."

He insisted that he should open the trunk, to take out the suitcases and to leave as quickly as possible from that place. They retrieved most of the ladies' luggage as well and took off at once down a path well off the road. Led by Phillip and his loved ones, without any specific direction yet, because Phillip just wanted to get them as far away from danger as possible, before deciding where to go. At the time he thought he was putting them in more danger by taking them with them than if he let them go on their own.

He knew that those who wanted to kill them did not know about them, and that was an important advantage that fate would give each one of them.

They walked for a long time until they reached a small town, which grew around a farm called San Javier, where they took refuge for a few hours. Phillip explained to them in detail the risk that being with them meant that it would be better if they let them go alone, so that they would not be in any danger.

Macedonio said that he knew someone who could help them, but he lived in a town a little far from where they were, so they had to find some means of transportation to get there. Socorro supported the idea of going to that town to seek help, so that Phillip and his family could flee the country without anyone noticing.

They all supported the idea of not leaving them alone, and that they would do everything possible to help them in any way, because of the gratitude they felt for having saved their lives.

Now they were on that path of pilgrimage and martyrdom, where each one would find their part among the plans of the divine. Phillip did not stop thinking about it with each step they took, but he was equally sure that they would guide them to the right place to continue.

Contemplating his new allies, Phillip wondered which one of them the divines influenced to support them along the way. Or if it was the case that was him who helped them to fulfill their missions or purposes. In any case, he felt that at no time they left them unprotected or helpless, despite the conditions in which they struggled.

They reached Viesca in a mule cart, which Macedonio bought with the money the inspector had asked him to take to the state capital. The road was very overwhelming due to the conditions of the region, and the time it took to get to that place, where the sand and desolation put everyone to the test.

The absence of external conflicts helped them rediscover their true selves, with their fears and dreams, with their religion and their faith. The only thing that could be heard on the way were the children talking about things that the older ones did not want to discuss, because they speculated about what had happened, and the reason why they had to leave the bus and travel in a mule cart. That reminded Phillip of Chendo's children, who always talked about things that adults prefer to avoid. "We should be like children," Phillip thought, at that moment when he listened to children teach adults to be like themselves.

The early morning brings a sense of hope for some, but for others, it seems cold and dark, despite the fact that it is a new opportunity granted from the highest spiritual realm, which guides us in every step of our existence.

Dawn lit up the desert as white as snow, blinding with its glimmers those unaccustomed to the light. They marveled at seeing the prevailing and promising sunrise over the salt desert, which would lead them to a new rebirth in their lives.

Macedonio took them to the camp of the salt miners who worked there and introduced them to the miners' foreman, who was a very good friend of his.

A red-skinned man named Arcadio Medina, introduced himself very cordially to everyone and promised to help them, after Macedonio and Phillip told him only a few things that they had agreed upon, so that he would not realize what had happened, and start to ask more about the matter. They agreed that it was better not to tell him anything about what had happened, to not put his life at risk as well.

Arcadio and Macedonio were very good friends, since they had attended the same elementary school, but they distanced themselves a bit when Macedonio's parents had to flee the town, due to the socialist ideas with which they managed to attract the attention of the capitalist government that ruled back then.

Sometime later in their teenage life, they managed to meet again when all the revolutionary uproar ended, and they were able to return to their hometown again.

They had to travel for another day in the mule cart until they reached a small town called Concordia, where they took refuge in the house of Arcadio's father for several days. But only while they agreed on what they wanted to do, or where they wanted to go.

Phillip had a gift in his favor that prevented him from certain events, the ability to perceive some possible results of what could happen. Not to see the future specifically, but to sense it as a possibility.

In that place they got rid of the anguish and worry of having to run away all the time, and they were finally able to rest from the torment of thinking about what had happened. Each one discovered something to occupy themselves while things settled on their own, so to speak, because they were already sure that nothing was random.

They soon discovered the solidarity and warmth of the good heart with which the people of the town received them, which caused each one to settle comfortably among that sincere welcome. Trust grew to the point of forming bonds that promised more than friendships.

After living together every day during those days, Arcadio invited Socorro to walk through the town square, so that she would not get bored locked up in the house. Socorro accepted very happily and asked him to wait a few minutes to change clothes and go for a walk with him. Phillip took advantage of the moment to talk to Arcadio about some matters. "Arcadio, from your blood a little hope will sprout in this world." Philip told him. Among other things he asked him to keep just for him, and that they would serve him at the right time, to overcome some difficulties that might arise in his life.

The afternoon walks in the town square fanned the flame of passion between Socorro and Arcadio, creating a custom that neither wanted to end; even though it was likely that they would not see each other again, in the event that Socorro's mother and her sister decided to leave for another town or return to their hometown.

At least, those were Arcadio's fears when he thought that he might lose the opportunity to enjoy her company. He could not allow that, under no circumstances could he let her go away, because he was in love with her from the first moment he saw her that morning in the salt desert, illuminated by the beauty of dawn and predestined just for him.

Phillip knew what fate had in store for them on their way, and he spoke to each one separately to advise them.

He felt the need and the obligation to help Socorro a little on her path of enlightenment, which will be inherited in her blood so what must be is fulfilled, so that one day the world could have a hope of love and freedom.

He told her that the divine were never wrong when choosing those who will guide the light of awakening. That she should feel proud and graceful for having the privilege of possessing the glory and the reason for the truth among her blood. He also warned her that all of this entailed a great responsibility of which she should be as prudent as possible so that the intention and the purpose were not lost, since evil would tempt some of her descendants to fall into falsehood and avarice. That protecting them and educating them in the path of goodness was her duty and her obligation as a protective mother.

Macedonio, after talking with Phillip about some issues that worried him about his faith, his way of seeing life, at least in the way he had been taught how reality is supposed to be in life, decided to go a little further to the north, to a small community of peasants that had been left behind in that region after the revolution.

He had a half-brother who had fought alongside the revolutionary general for many years, and he had lost the opportunity to live with him, because he had to go fight for freedom, almost as a child. He knew that it was the opportunity to meet his brother again and live with him the time they never had, to recover the moments that fate had taken from them.

"There in La Victoria I'll settle down, then." He told Phillip in one of their conversations.

Phillip congratulated him on how brave he had been that night when they had to flee from the murderers, and on the way he had embraced all that spirituality and awakening. He also told him that, within a certain time, he would have to act so that they could never find the trace of any of those who got off the passenger bus; furthermore, he insisted that he be diligent in his attempt to discover doubts but not be confused by external noise or the vanity of desires that are suggested in the hearts of the living.

That all the answers to his doubts would be found within his heart.

One Thursday at noon he left Concordia to go to La Victoria, in search of the lost moments with his brother, to start a new life in that place, where he would find love and his vocation as a farmer.

Arcadio formally asked Socorro's mother for permission to take her to the festival that took place every November twenty, commemorating the town's anniversary, so he asked everyone to accompany them. He told them that they could not miss it, since it was a celebration in which all the people participated.

Arcadio felt from his heart that they were already part of such town, just as Socorro was already part of his heart.

Phillip felt that this was not the time for celebrations, because of the anguish he had been thinking about what he should do to keep his family as far away as possible from the miserable murderers, who would try to find them and kill them just to hide the truth.

After Arcadio convinced him that they would not have any risk of anything, Phillip agreed, acknowledging that no one knew them in that town and that there was a very low possibility that they would know their whereabouts, after what had happened that night when they escaped from the bus.

He remembered that the criminal had reported to his boss that they had all been killed; Therefore, they would believe that they had died that night, and there was no possibility that they would know that they were still alive, or that they would know their identity. That gave him some confidence to at least consider that maybe were safe for this occasion.

Even so, after kindly accepting Arcadio's invitation, he knew that the manipulators of the truth had their malicious weapons to look for what interests them, and they would not stop for any reason if they knew that someone had in their possession any of The Tools of Order.

He knew that, just as the divine had their chosen, the wicked had some manipulated to cooperate in their quest for power. Some puppets twisted by ambition and confusion of the spirit. Chosen with the right gifts, but who have been deceived or forced to contribute evil.

For now, Phillip knew that he would have time to relax a bit and take a walk with Elida and Emma through the town, knowing that one day the town would play an important role in the resurgence of truth and order, by Moonlight, in her return to save love from the clutches of the manipulator, who takes advantage of some locals to achieve his goal.

Elida dressed Emma in the dress she had made together with her grandmother, so that she would take part in the pageant for the queen of the town. Arcadio had suggested it the moment he saw her as radiant as a jewel at dawn, with that beautiful dress worthy of royalty.

Emma was taken to each of the amusement rides that were around the town square, plus many more rides that people put up along the streets. There were all kinds of food everywhere, brought by the richest families in town for people to eat at no cost.

Also, many people brought tables outside the door of their house, so that those who did not have to eat would come and celebrate next to them.

The entire town celebrated the founding of Concordia with great joy, in an atmosphere of solidarity and kindness that Phillip had not seen until that day. That filled his heart with great pride and respect for the people of that Shire town.

Arcadio took advantage of the moment of joy that everyone was going through to tell them some good news, when they were eating in the middle of the town square. He got up from his chair and drawing the attention of all those present who could hear him, he said that he had a very important proposition to make to a person who had illuminated his life. At that moment he approached Socorro, and kneeling in front of her, he asked her to marry him. Socorro jumped on top of him, kissing him and telling him yes, that nothing else would make her happier in life. Socorro's mother and her sister cried with happiness, hugging the children who also cried, seeing the love that they radiated from each other in the middle of the town square. All the people celebrated with great joy at the news that Arcadio would finally get married, since everyone knew him very well for his noble and simple character.

The participants from the region gathered around the fountain, which was in the center of the town square, for the award ceremony, where the farmers built a throne for the winner to sit on. Without a doubt, that was Emma, as she unanimously won the vote for her charisma and beauty, which was further highlighted by that beautiful dress worthy of a queen. "Premonitions of fate," thought Phillip, at the moment when the town judge placed the crown on her head and handed her the little scepter they had made at the last minute. "God bless queen Emma!" People were screaming.

_jema_sid

Chapter 4
The Reconciliation

They walked her through the streets of the town, sitting on the throne built by the farmers, which they put in a truck decorated with all kinds of details and flowers everywhere. Arcadio drove the truck accompanied by Socorro, the woman who would be his life and his love.

All the townspeople threw flowers at them as they passed by their houses, and shouted blessings for the new queen. Emma saw with great affection all beings that admired her tenderness and grace, as well as blessing them with those broken words from her first age.

No one could deny that that innocent light of love deserved to be the queen of the people, realizing her beauty and her splendor of justice and reason. Phillip was surprised at how much the people loved and admired her, which made him think about the glorious future of that region, when they received the liberator of conscience. He knew that it would have to happen a long time before that could be possible, and that it was also possible that it would never happen, due to the evil with which the world is deceived by injustice and lies.

Those days helped the friendship between Elida and Socorro, as well as with her mother Sofia Ceniceros, and her sister Guadalupe Ceniceros.

Elida told them about those days when they lived in the dump, and how they had managed to free the people from the executioner who devastated the entire region with his threats of hate. She was about to tell them about what had happened with the death of her uncle, but she felt that perhaps she would put them in a very serious risk by telling them some things, so she had to modify a bit the version of how it had happened all that. She also told them about her grandmother and her great friend Mama Chayo, whom she loved as if she were her mother.

Mrs. Sofia Ceniceros gave her condolences for the loss of her uncle, at the moment when she gave her the blessing so that God would heal her sorrows.

She asked her to be strong to overcome her pain, and she gave her a gold chain with a silver earring that her grandmother had given her.

"Now you will need it more, sweetheart," she told her, "Take it and always keep it close to your chest."

Elida was very happy to have their help during her stay in that town. That if it were up to her, she would stay to live forever, but she knew that they should leave as soon as possible to the north, in search of their own destiny as a family.

The memory of Mama Chayo and her great friend Inés invaded her when she felt that affection that Mrs. Sofia and her daughters shared with her. Although the occasion was somewhat ephemeral, she managed to enjoy next to them that feeling of peace and harmony that she feels at home.

She could not help but miss those afternoons in the mansion's garden, while she enjoyed the sunset next to her grandmother and her soulmates. She missed them with tears in her eyes on many occasions, although she kept the hope that she could come back one day to continue enjoying their love.

In a certain way, she also felt the premonitions of destiny just like Phillip, that is why she knew that her place would be next to her daughter and her lover until the last moment of her life.

The little girl named Genoveva gave Emma a loving hug and told her that they would see each other again one day. That she loved her very much; then she kissed her. She stood in front of Elida and Mrs. Sofia, and with that sympathy of innocence that sometimes characterizes children, she said, "Grandma Sofia, this could be the beginning of what you were referring to."

That innocence had brought tears to her mother and grandmother, because of the truth of her words, but also because the little girl was right, and they knew it.

Little Genoveva and Emma danced in the middle of the room, at the moment when the girl said that they would see each other again to celebrate freedom together. "Yeah!" Shouted Moonlight. "And one day we will all celebrate together!" Genoveva shouted, while they danced holding hands, illuminated by the sunlight coming through the window.

Elida carefully observed the moment to not miss any detail, at the suggestion of Phillip, who knew how important those details were to appreciate the unrepeatable moments that life gives us.

For that and for some reason that she sensed, it is why she did not stop enjoying every second next to those beautiful beings that the creator put in her path. Although she was not blinded to the fate that she rushed without remedy or mercy on them. "Premonitions of destiny," Elida thought, seeing her daughter and Genoveva holding hands dancing with joy, celebrating an event that had not yet happened.

In the midst of all that joy and coexistence, Elida thought about those visions that sometimes tormented her, but even so she hoped that in the end everything would turn out as her heart longed for. Not knowing that fate or the universe had prepared something unique for them. With an uncertain path, but with incomparable glory and light, so it was well worth a try.

During the days that they stayed in the town of Concordia, Genoveva taught Emma to say a lot of words, as well as the vowels. A very special reciprocal love had grown in them, which would transcend beyond what any man could ever imagine; Well, it is love, the key to free the truth from all things that cause confusion in the world of the living, fears and incapacities for self-growth and healing.

These qualities that awaken the spirit from this sublime dream of modern reality are recognized today by every human being on the planet, but they are not practiced patiently enough to realize that this is the true path that the spirit desires.

Each one examines yourself carefully to know what you need.

Good values, respect, and honesty, as well as decency and empathy towards this whole beautiful universe in which we all live, are just an example of some of these qualities that we all possess, but that we often let go unnoticed due to confusing noise that the media shapes in our minds.

The vicissitudes that teach us pain are as necessary as those that teach us joy and love; therefore, the contrast must be balanced so that the spirit can understand the difference between the duality of our existence; the nature of our physical state in this world, as well as the truth of its origin as consciousness.

It is necessary for each one of us to seek to understand and assimilate every quality that helps us rediscover our true personal purpose, in order to be able to release any ties that could keep us in ignorance and fear, in order to truly live in freedom.

Three days after the festival, they left Concordia to go on to the north in Arcadio's father's old truck, who took them to a nearby town, and where they took refuge for a day in the house of one of his cousins, before getting back on their way to try to cross the border without anyone noticing. Because it was not convenient for them to cross with the permits the grandmother had gotten for them, because that would be an easy trail for those who was trying to kill them. Besides, it was likely that Elida's stepfather already knew about them, and he might try to follow them to harm them.

Phillip decided that they should cross illegally so there would not be records of their names, so no one would know where they had gone. He had not yet realized the power that these greedy had in the world and was unaware of the extent of their miserable petty interests.

They said goodbye in the afternoon after chatting a little more about some things and details that Phillip had told him about some things that could happen to him in the future. At the end, Arcadio gave them a hug, and a kiss on Emma's forehead.

"I know we'll see each other again," Arcadio told them.

"That's right," Phillip answered, "farewell."

Due to the inconveniences that had happened, Elida and Phillip had not had time to resume their nightly talks, until that night, when they finally had the opportunity to talk about what was best for little Moonlight.

They stayed in a small room that Arcadio's cousin had given them, where there was only a cot and a couple of blankets, so they had to huddle Emma between them so she would not get cold, because in that region the coldness was much crueler at that time of year.

At midnight, Phillip woke up feeling a strange sensation in his stomach, which made him get up to meditate a bit on what was happening to him, because he was not sure if he was dreaming or if something was about to happen. He stood in front of the window where the moonlight came in, illuminating Elida and Emma where they were lying.

Elida had woken up when she felt Phillip getting up, but she did not say anything until she looked at him worriedly staring at the moon.

"What is it, Quixote?" Elida asked.

"Not yet." Phillip answered.

"We'll be fine, don't worry, my love," Elida insisted. "Come back here you must rest."

"I don't know if that's what will happen," he stared into her eyes. "I am afraid of failing."

Elida reminded him of the love she felt for him, and the favor that the divine had for them, who would protect them from anything, regardless of the place or time.

He went back to the cot with his loved ones to try to get some sleep, but after three and a half hours he suddenly woke up with the same feeling of anguish and discomfort that would not let him sleep. He got up again to look at the moon in the middle of the morning, which was shining brighter than usual.

Suddenly he was lost in the midst of the visions that assailed him at the moment, leaving him immobile for a few minutes, until Elida spoke to him to ask him what was wrong with him.

At that moment, Phillip returned from his visions more anguished than before, worried about what he could not do if he lost his life, because he would not be able to help his loved ones in any way afterwards. Still, he was willing to give his life for them, if it meant they would be okay.

"I'm fine honey, don't worry," Phillip told her, "I'll watch over you until the day comes.

Elida told him that she was fine, but that he should try to get some rest as well, since the day would be difficult. Phillip knew it, but he also had matters to consider first with himself, before facing his fate once more.

Elida tried to fall asleep hugging Moonlight towards her chest, to prevent the mystical cold of those morning hours from disturbing her dreams. She could not sleep because of the worry she felt at not knowing how to help her beloved, with the weight that the divine design had placed on her shoulders, by choosing him to carry out the difficult task of defending truth and love. Elida did not know that she had already done it, in the most extraordinary way she had helped him to get out of his zone of conformity; above all by truly loved him. Because it was not until Phillip could see behind Elida's eyes that he fell in love with her; that is how he knew her true love by seeing the same light in the eyes of the fruit of their love, Moonlight. Thanks to that love that Phillip discovered in them, Phillip rediscovered the meaning of life and death. Before, he only lived conditioned to the world where the powerful manage the fate of the population, unable to escape the injustice of inequality and indifference.

The first rays of the morning sun entered through the window illuminating Elida and Emma, at the moment when Phillip saw them with the fear of losing them. He could not explain why they had to go through all that happened to them, despite knowing that the path of the chosen ones is like that, full of stones and thorns, pain, and tears.

He grumbled a little when he saw his loved ones with the discomfort of suffering because of him, but he did not flinch in any way when he thought that his purpose was much greater than any vanity or ego. He took a deep breath to gather strength from his heart, so he could face whatever was about to happen. The good morning of his beloved daughter and the smile of his beloved Elida filled him with determination.

Phillip heard some noise in the corral of the house, and he thought that it was Arcadio's cousin preparing the cart that would take them to the crossing point. He realized it when he heard him fight with the mule, trying to put it in the cart.

He told Elida that he would go help him and that he would be back in a moment; for which Elida told him that it was fine, that they would get up in a moment to get ready to leave. Phillip told her not to worry, that he would first go and agree with Arcadio's cousin on the details of when they would leave, then he would return to inform her. She agreed, and she reminded him how much she loved him, as Phillip kissed Emma on her forehead. "I love you too, skinny." Philip told them.

All those afternoons when they went hunting in Chendo's cart, his best friend and compadre, helped him learn the art of saddling and placing the mule in the cart, which is why he suggested to Arcadio's cousin some techniques that would help him to do it better and faster. Fidencio, as the tall man with reddish-brown skin was called, replied that he did not need his help, because he had everything under control. That the mule got very reticent in those hours of the morning, so he already knew its tricks. Phillip insisted in the kindest way possible to allow him to show him even once, but Fidencio was reluctant to let Phillip teach him how to do it, since he did it that way every day. There was no way to make him change his mind, Phillip realized that, recognizing in Fidencio the same stubbornness that he himself had faced on some occasion.

Knowing that Fidencio would not accept his help, either way, Phillip approached the mule while Fidencio was trying to push her on the cart. He touched her on the chest, and the mule suddenly calmed down, while Phillip spoke to her telling her not to worry because he would protect her.

The mule stared at Phillip with her neck lowered, then put her head on Phillip's shoulder, closed her eyes and sighed. Phillip hugged her by her neck and the mule shed a tear, which fell on Phillip's cheek.

"Calm down, don't be afraid," Phillip told the mule, "I know that we have been unfair to you by not knowing how to listen to you."

Fidencio had remained motionless observing what was happening, not knowing what to say or what to do; Well, at the moment the mule was crying, he was overwhelmed by a great feeling of guilt, which made him cry.

"Bencho didn't want to hurt you," Phillip told the mule, "He did not know."

Fidencio, upon hearing that Phillip called him Bencho, asked Phillip how he knew what his relatives called him, that if it had been Arcadio who told him, because he did not like being called that, while he was drying his tears and trying to recover his rude stance.

"She told me," Phillip told him, "she knows your name." While he hugged the mule by the neck.

Fidencio fell to his knees looking at the sky, crying and asking God for forgiveness for how unfair he had been to that innocent being, to forgive him out of mercy. Phillip saw that his repentance was sincere, and asked Fidencio to stand up so that he could approach the mule and talk to her; for she would listen to him if he spoke to her with a true heart.

With tears streaming down his face, Fidencio approached the mule and hugged her neck, begging her to forgive him for how unfair he had been to her. The mule put her head on Fidencio's shoulder, closed her eyes and sighed, as a sign that everything was fine between the two of them.

For the first time in a long time, Fidencio felt that he was alive, which is why he recognized how blind he had been to that noble being, especially to the injustice and ignorance in which many of us live deceived. He promised to be fair and respectful to her so that she would not suffer anymore because of him, and he wiped her tears with his own hands, in the same way that he wiped his own tears.

Elida had left the room at the moment when all this was happening, holding Emma in her arms, observing the example that life sets for our bones and aching flesh, to learn the lesson that will help us grow as spirits.

Emma asked Elida to put her down and walked a few steps to where Fidencio was hugging the mule. The mule reacted by turning to see Emma, who was raising her hand to greet that poor innocent being, smiling at him with that face of an angel of light. Moonlight walked a few steps towards her, for which Phillip asked Fidencio to wait a bit, which

Fidencio did without asking. The mule turned around, walked towards the cart, and positioned herself to be tied up, which caught Fidencio's attention, in such a way that he approached it to kiss her neck. He told her how good she was to him and that he loved her very much, then he respectfully tied her up, without any discriminatory abuse or sadism, so they could leave as soon as possible and get to the crossing point on time.

They left at six thirty in the morning, after having prepared something to eat for the road, thanks to the fact that Fidencio shared some of the little he had in his small and humble adobe kitchen.

It could be said that Fidencio had experienced an awakening from the dream that life had formed in him, recognizing that his actions were wrong, that his intentions were misunderstood; for this reason, he changed his position as a brusque and ill-faced man, when he felt the truth of universal love among all beings of creation, at the moment of reconciliation between him and the mule, which for many years had served him without receiving some kind of gratitude.

They came to some shacks that Fidencio had inherited from his grandfather, to rest a bit from the cold that was felt more and more as the days passed. This worried Phillip and Elida a lot, because of the risk that Emma would get sick from walking from one place to the other, so they insisted to Fidencio that they should cross as soon as possible, before it began to freeze at night. Fidencio told them not to worry, that the day after tomorrow during afternoon they would cross, because he already had everything planned with one of his friends, who would take them to a small town on the other side of the border, where they could stay as long as they wanted while they decided what to do or where to go.

In all that time it took them to reach the dividing line, Phillip talked with Fidencio about some details about the path his life could take, if he did not pay attention to certain details that would unexpectedly appear on his way.

Fidencio took every piece of advice that Phillip gave him with great respect, for which he felt grateful for having helped him, realizing the misunderstanding that kept him enslaved in indifference. Now he was committed to sharing that feeling that he had discovered in him, and which he did not know he had. His determination was firmer than his pride or his vanity, for now the rudeness of his ignorance no longer blinded him, that is why he bare his being without fear to receive the light of truth and the reason for justice. Now he was free, now he was in control of his life.

A few hours after they left, they arrived at Charcos de Risa, where with the help of a friend they took them to Cuatro Ciénegas, in a truck they used to haul cows. They rested in a log cabin, which Fidencio's friend had built to take his family on vacation each year. Not for long, because Phillip insisted that they should leave as soon as possible, so they just took care of their basic necessities and got ready to head north again.

Fidencio talked with his friend about some details of what had happened to him, so that he would understand a little why he wanted to help them, being complete strangers to him. Upon hearing his way of speaking and the way he referred to Phillip and his loved ones, Fidencio's friend was surprised by what he heard, because he knew him very well, and he knew that he was not like that. He felt very proud that finally someone had made him see the dark side of him, but he felt happier knowing that Fidencio had accepted his faults.

There is nothing more welcoming than feeling the hug of a friend when you feel ashamed, that is a respect and feeling that many of us know.

Ever since Arcadio's grandfather had taught him to drive, he and Fidencio visited him in the summer to go to the horse races in Cuatro Ciénegas. Amador Bernal was the name of that nice young man with a cheerful posture and a simple heart, who had also attended the same school as them when he was a child. Before leaving again, Fidencio showed Amador a map to see which route would be the safest to get to Minas, since he did not want them to take the main road that led to Monclova.

Phillip approached them to help them a bit with his experience, but Amador knew the place much better than anyone, so he suggested a route that he knew quite well. Phillip agreed with Amador about the route they should follow, as if he knew that mysterious passage, which they set out to take after agreeing on the stopping points.

Fidencio suggested to Amador that he trust what Phillip told him, so that he would not deviate from what they had agreed for any reason, and that he decides at that moment if he wanted to continue helping them.

Amador, knowing that his life might be in danger, kindly agreed to continue, since he appreciated his great friend very much. And seeing him so animated and involved in his efforts to help Phillip and his family, he immediately helped them load the suitcases into the truck, and some backpacks with something to eat for the road.

Phillip knew that it would take them longer than Fidencio had estimated to reach the border of the country. That worried him, because the cold was felt much more among the hills, and he feared that this would be an impediment for them to pass without setbacks.

In Minas they put fuel, in addition to putting some air in a spare tire, which was at the gas station near a corner. Then, they left immediately to not waste any more time so they can reach Morelos before sunset.

On the way from Morelos to San Carlos, Phillip felt a strange sensation in his belly, which made him worry a little, believing that something was going to happen, but at the moment he wanted to say something, he had a very confused vision of a very cold and dark place., where he could see himself lying on the ground mortally wounded. At that moment he could see The Old Lady with the White Hair behind him, with the spear in her hand, aiming right at his head. He could not see more details since he had to come back from time to time to not worry Elida about his reaction.

She knew what was happening to him because she knew him well, and because of that characteristic instinct of women that is more acute in mothers, to feel and sense things that could happen to their loved ones.

Elida got close to him to put his head on her shoulder and give him some comfort, leaving Emma sheltered next to the suitcases, on a cot that Arcadio had given them.

"I'm fine," Phillip told her. "Don't worry skinny."

More than anything, he did to not worry her more than she already was. Because of that stress that caused having to run away to save their life all the time, and without knowing how or when.

Elida was aware of what could possibly happen, having that heavenly gift that is sharpened in mothers by presenting things that men have no idea. Above all, having the privilege of guiding and supporting the one chosen by the divine, to continue courageously and without fear on that uncertain path full of bitterness and worries.

We all know that famous saying that goes, "Behind a great man there is always a great woman."

Something in their favor was that Phillip had that heavenly gift, which anticipates in advance what could happen at a certain moment, and that would help them to take advantage of the enemy at the right moment, at the right time.

She was not disadvantaged by the divine either, being the one who held the burden of protecting love and reason from justice, among the cold indifference and ingratitude with which many men contaminate their hearts. Without a doubt, together they were much stronger than they thought. Each one put their grain of sand to build the path and the foundations of the home they dreamed of one day. Elida returned and took Moonlight in her arms, snuggled her against her chest and told Phillip that they would be fine, not to worry. That this was not the time to tell him, but that she felt within herself that everything would turn out according to the plans that the Creator had drawn up for their destinies. And that in the end, the purpose would be revealed to the chosen ones to help others with the truth. Phillip knew her just as she knew him; as such, he knew that she had a higher gift than him, and he trusted that she was right, even knowing that it would cost them their life's.

Phillip recognized that the purpose was greater than the time period of human life on this planet, compared to the timelessness of the spirit. He approached them and hugged them crying with happiness, for that chance of life in putting them together as a family, as a special team with similar feelings. "I don't know how to name you, but thank you for allowing me this moment," Phillip thought, at the moment when his heart radiated a strange energy that covered the three of them, which made their hair stand on end, but which it would keep them sheltered from the cold and the wind until they reached the dividing line.

Chapter 5
The Covenant Of The Divine

They crossed the border the following afternoon in a small raft that a friend of Amador's had provided them in San Carlos.

Amador told his friend that they wanted to go fishing in the lagoon, because an acquaintance and his family had visited him, so he wanted to show them around.

The friend thought it was strange that Amador did not bring his family with him, but even so he did not ask him anything about it. He lent him the raft on the condition that they return the next day because he wanted to accompany them, since he was busy at the time with some business in the village dispensary.

Amador promised him that they would return early for him, and they would go to the lagoon to compete who would be the best fisherman, to get ready because he would not give him any respite this time. His friend accepted the challenge and promised him that he would not give him a chance either, that he better stop bragging because he would only end up crying with shame like last time.

That was the last afternoon in which they had the privilege of stepping on the land where they were born, so the universe sent them off with that flushed sunset, so that they never want to leave. Despite realizing how the universe was trying to persuade them of what might possibly await them when they crossed the border, they crossed the Rio Bravo at nightfall that even the fish did not notice.

As if everything was ready for them to cross without any setbacks, or without adversity preventing what the divine had already decided. Nobody could do anything about it, because even the powerful and corrupt must bow to the will of the Creator.

Amador took Phillip and his family to El Quemado, where he took them to a house of a relative who lived across the street from the town's Baptist church. They stayed there for a few days so they could rest from the trip and could think carefully about what they wanted to do next.

At El Quemado Phillip met a friend of Amador's cousin, who visited her in the afternoons on certain days. They had grown up together in that community, and they had never ceased to seek each other as friends, despite the fact that each one already had their own family. There was no romance between them, only sincere friendship; Well, whoever knows a good friend knows that sometimes his or her help seems more faithful and welcoming than the family.

Eleonor Bernal, as that fair-skinned woman with a sweet character was called, served as a volunteer helping with disabled children at the town school. She gave them art and meditation classes in the mornings, and in the afternoons, she sometimes visited them at their homes to bring them some food and toys; In addition to taking advantage of the visit to speak with the children's relatives on how to approach them when caring for them, according to the conditions that each child had.

Her great friend, John Bonham, who was a simple guy with a very broad criteria, spoke with Phillip about the adventures of his life, while Eleonor laughed at the nonsense that her great friend recounted.

"Conspiracies," Eleonor told him.

"They're not conspiracies," John told her. "What it is, is that you are stupid as a mule."

Eleonor did not agree with the conspiratorial ideas that John told Phillip, as she was a woman who was very sure of her convictions and her beliefs. She did not accept the idea that there are beings from other worlds living among us, without people realizing it.

Phillip listened carefully to what that idealistic guy talked about his experiences with these beings from other worlds, and the way they manipulated everyone's lives.

Eleonor asked Phillip if he believed the crazy things that his friend was talking about, convinced that Phillip would not support such nonsense.

"Perhaps, not believing that it is possible is one of their tricks that serve in their favor." Philip answered.

Eleonor burst out laughing when she heard Phillip support John with his crazy ways, so she turned to Elida asking her if she could believe what these crazy couple were saying. Elida was not surprised, nor did she reflect disagreement on what she had just heard from John.

She stared at Eleonor for a few seconds, until Eleonor stopped laughing at the way Elida was looking at her, then she took a breath and sighed.

Eleonor realized that Elida was trying to tell her something when she saw the light in her eyes, which made her doubt what was really happening. But she still remained skeptical about those crazy ideas that her friend always said. She refused to accept an idea different from how she had been brought up, since her religious belief did not allow the freedom of her conscience, limiting her openness to only some radical ideas. Still, her spirit was free from greed or vanity, from covetousness or envy.

Elida asked her to accompany her to the room to see the clothes she had given her for little Emma, and so they could talk a little more about it.

Eleonor followed her somewhat disconcerted by the mysterious light that she had seen in Elida, but she was indifferent, talking about the children at school and the way in which the one and mighty God cared for them, not wanting to broach again that subject that disturbed her. Elida realized Eleonor's discomfort, seeing her talk about the children, and seeing how her pride in her chest did not let her breathe. Especially because of the way she avoided her gaze at all times. Elida asked her to look into her eyes, and told her that she was no Medusa, that she would not turn her to stone. Besides, she was a woman, which would not work with her. They both laughed at the same time at what Elida had said, and the topic that she was worried about had left her mind as she felt the confidence that Elida reflected in her gaze.

They had a good time talking about endless things, while Phillip finished talking with John about their experiences in life.

Elida told her about her grandmother, how they spent the afternoons knitting jackets for the children and doing all kinds of crafts. How she enjoyed listening to her sing, since the grandmother had been part of a group called Los Mirlos, in her younger years. She told her that her grandmother took a nap after dinner, then she got up to go to the garden to water the plants and trees, singing all the time those beautiful songs; the same ones that she sang to her as a child before going to sleep.

Eleonor was a noble woman with a good heart, it was not difficult for her to earn Elida's trust, nor Emma's affection; Well, if there was something that she did best in life, it was to help the children and to love them with all her heart.

There was no malice in her, nor obsession for aberrations deeply rooted in the subconscious; Well, neither greed nor envy had taken over her ideals, nor her goals as a person.

Voluntary service reflects the true nature of the spirit. That nature was intensely reflected in her actions of nobility, in the church helping the elderly to sit at the desks, likewise as in the daily dealings with others, who formed her work environment, or daily dedication, and almost aberration for wanting to help those poor disabled children. I could hang a thousand more attributes on her that would define her a bit as the excellent person she was. In those days Elida helped her a little with the housework, while Eleonor went to serve at the school. And on some afternoons when she went to help clean the church during non-service hours. Eleanor had done it every day for many years, ever since her eldest son had been killed in the war.

Without a doubt, it had had a great impact on her life and her faith. Even so, she never formed a reproach against God for having taken her son, nor for having allowed her husband to take his life, learning that their son had died.

Eleonor had taken refuge in the idea within her heart, that there was a paradise in heaven where her loved ones would rest to ease their pain, and that God would take care of them, just as she would if she had the chance.

Everyone judge in your own way whatever you have to deal with yourself, so you can transcend a little more in the search for the truth, with a nobler heart, and a more complete wisdom about what is correct in life and love.

John was an electrical engineer and worked for several years for the county power supply company, having worked for the military since he had graduated from college, on different projects in different states across the nation. He liked classical music and discussing the philosophy of Plato's Republic. He always bored his viewers with his talks about conspiracies that the world government invented to manipulate the population, which caused people to ignore him and judge him as a deranged madman.

Phillip understood the helpless feeling John felt when people ignored him, because he felt the same way trying to tell others about his experiences.

Experiences that could well serve so that same people could take advantage of the lesson that others have already learned and apply it in their lives. Phillip had understood a long time ago that it was not about telling everyone about what we experience in our daily life , but to transmit with our daily acts in our daily routine, the intentions that the spirit learned in its realization.

Their friendship grew every day, not because they coincided in their ideals, but because of the good heart they both had and the nobility that was reflected in all their attributes, by sharing with other living beings the life that had been entrusted to them.

It was obvious that their spirits had more strength and intelligence than others, due to the wisdom that their actions reflected in the service they were always willing to render, without expecting any recognition that would show off their vanity a bit.

John's great-grandfather had emigrated from Scotland a little over a century ago, bringing his family with him. Months after checking into Clinton Castle, along with his wife and two children, they decided to migrate a little further south in search of the promised land, which had been revealed to John's great-great-grandfather in a vision at the time just before dying.

The story was kept as a tradition in the family, and with the passing of time the date was celebrated, in commemoration of the first foundation that John's great-grandfather had made, and other emigrants who decided to settle in that place to sow their dreams, which bore fruit that fed many without anyone having the idea of the truth.

John had left the community after graduating from college as an electrical engineer, to work in the army as an officer in charge of top-secret war projects. According to what he always said in his endless speeches.

He had ended up in El Quemado because he had married a beautiful young woman native to that land, who totally blessed him by giving him two beautiful children, who reflected with their way of being the character of love and respect that they were taught at home. This pair of gentle beings accompanied their father very often to talk with

Phillip, when they had time in the afternoons after work and school; Well, after school they worked in the town's carpentry shop as helpers. They did not get a penny for their work, but they did it wholeheartedly because of the great intention they had of learning a new trade every year. They were just as crazy as their father, just as lucid and intelligent, and they were not so easily fooled by any nursery tale.

They had the gift of understanding things a little deeper than any of us because the universe had wanted it that way, according to what John told Phillip in his evening talks. They were very noble kids, who always asked permission very cordially and with a big smile before giving their opinion on anything. Always waiting for the right moment so as to not to interrupt in the middle of the conversation to the person who was speaking.

They knew that their father was not a liar, nor a charlatan who dedicated himself to manipulating people with his tales of distant worlds and stellar life.

In a certain way, they supported the ideas that their father told them about the immensity of worlds in the galaxy, where different expressions of life lived, with characteristics and shapes according to the conditions of each world. Even so, they kept a certain margin of criticism regarding everything they were told, and they shared the belief that there was a strong possibility that all of this was a mere fantasy created by their father to keep them entertained as children, and that at some point it had turned into a conditioned truth.

Phillip remembered his compadre Chendo's children, listening to those lucid and well-educated pair of cherubs speak. He remembered the afternoons when they would go hunting, and the children would talk about almost anything as if they knew the answers to all of them.

Phillip felt that his mission was about to end in that place, so he should prepare to leave as soon as possible, because he wanted to reach the place where his visions were concentrated, in order to discover the reason why that place was so special for his family.

He had a presentiment of some things that tormented him because he did not know clearly what it was about, but he also knew that it was essential for him to venture out in order to fulfill the task that the divine placed on his shoulders, using him as an essential tool in this crowded world of injustice and hatred, in order to free the innocent from the bitter slavery with which they are deceived and tormented.

He was sure that he had an important mission to carry out, not only in this world, but among the stars. That was a mystery he was willing to uncover no matter what the means or how.

The only thing that worried him was the pain that he could cause by his obligation to his loved ones, but he also knew that this was inevitable. Besides that, it was necessary for everything to happen in a certain way for him to understand the lesson properly, otherwise he would be a total failure.

He told Elida in their nocturnal talks, some things that John told him about his work, in addition to the crazy things he always said about the life that existed among the stars.

She always listened to him with great attention, respecting his opinion very serenely about what Phillip told her, but she would interrupt him if she had something to say, either because she differed from his opinions, or because she agreed.

On one of those nights, Phillip realized that she did not want to say a word about it, which is why her concerned attitude seemed strange to him when she heard the subject.

"What's going on skinny?"

"It's an anguish in my belly, I don't know what to do," she thought for a bit, and told him. "I don't know how to tell you, but there are voices out there calling for my help, but I don't know how to help them."

94

Phillip hugged her tightly against his chest, while she cried because of the impotence she felt at not knowing how to help those poor souls.

She cried as much as she had to, until she felt relief at the thought that she could at least help those around her. And that, perhaps, that was the answer that she was trying to find in the midst of her anguish of not knowing what to do. Little Emma, hearing her mother cry, got out of bed, and walked towards her with open arms, calling her. "Mom, mom." Emma told her with the same cry that hurt her mother inside, because she also felt it in her chest when she saw her cry with anguish.

Melted in the mystical embrace of love, for those who suffer the inevitable and inexpressible pain of others, they formed the unrepeatable moment, where a kind of energy began to emanate mysteriously surrounding the three of them, which was similar to the energy that Phillip had experienced in the chapel of Father Joaquín.

Phillip took Emma in his arms, and the two of them hugged Elida while she was still whimpering. She was comforted to see and feel how they welcomed her in her arms, with unconditional and unmeasured love from the most loved ones in her life.

The energy became more pleasant when each one realized in their being that being together was the most important thing as a family; Well, they had each other. Above all, at times when the soul suffers more from anguish than the vicissitudes of life put us to the test.

That same night they planned the next step in their mission, to be better prepared in case something was about to happen, because the gift they both had made them even stronger than they imagined. They began to share their concerns regarding the things that each had discovered in their visions, to form a better idea of how and where certain events would take place. Each one had certain visions regarding what disturbed them in their soul, and they did not come together in a sequential clarity, far from it. These visions differed in time and place from one another; at least, at that moment it was what they both recognized.

Eleonor was somewhat sad when she found out that they had decided to leave, because she had grown very fond of them in that short time in which she had humbly offered them her house. Elida's sympathy and modesty had captivated Eleonor's attention; perhaps, trying to fill the void that she had left after losing her family. She gave them her blessing and told them that she would support them in whatever they decided to do, because she would always count on her friendship.

Elida had told Eleonor some reasons why they could not stay for a long time, but without telling her too many details, so that she would not risk her life by learning more about them; furthermore, that due to circumstances that man cannot understand, they would have to flee as far as possible from certain petty creatures, and those who persecuted them to kill them.

At first Eleonor did not understand what she was saying about those loveless creatures, nor the reasons they had for wanting to kill them.

It was her daily contact with Elida and little Moonlight, which made her change her mind about some things, to which some of us do not pay attention, and which go beyond any concept of thought. Eleonor knew that there had always been wicked people who persecuted the children of God in order to kill them, and she knew that evil would not rest until it managed to finish with the light of truth.

She understood when she saw them leave in John's car, at the moment of feeling loneliness again, wanting to capture her in a state of sadness and abandonment.

The truth of what she had understood while living with them comforted her with hope in her heart, and the tears of sadness for parting turned to joy, well then, she understood that the only thing she could offer them was the desire in her heart that God would always bless them in their way.

Phillip had agreed with John to take them to the Crystal City, where they would meet one of his friends to help them get to La Victoria, where some distant relatives of his lived. John had written a letter to his relatives asking them to help Phillip and his family with whatever they could. That he thanked them in advance and was confident that soon he would be able to see them and live a little like when they were children.

Phillip said goodbye to his good friend and his two children, giving each of them a couple of pieces of advice so that they would never let evil confuse their noble heart.

They were very strong spirited beings, even so, they appreciated the advice of that humble man who only tried to call them to action to protect the truth.

With one hand he touched the book and with the other he blessed them. They hugged them at the end and told them that they hoped they would visit again one day. Emma took them by the cheeks with her hands and kissed the forehead of each one, at the moment when she blessed them and told them that she loved them very much.

Elida also gave them a hug and a kiss on their cheek. She told them that they were so lucky to have each other, that they would never let adversity and deceit separate them. They promised to be good.

The friend who had taken them to La Victoria had not found John's relatives, nor anyone who could give them any news of them. It seemed as if no one knew them, or that they had never lived in that place. This greatly worried Phillip and Elida, who suspected an evil doing, so that nothing would go well for them._Who could deny what is known by all, that when trying to do something good, there is always an equal or greater opposing force to prevent the task from being carried out.

The closer you get to the good, the greater the response of the dark will be to prevent you from achieving your goals. Despite this, you should not break your hope that if you persist in working on your dreams of doing good, sooner or later you will achieve it. Do not stop.

Not knowing what to do, he went to one of his trusted friends, who was dedicated to trading objects used in voodoo rites, some species of medicinal plants and magical amulets. Hoping that he could help them find shelter, they set off in search of him.

A medium-sized, dark-skinned as night man named Low Burnett, greeted them cheerfully with a big smile on his face, arms outstretched holding an amulet in each hand.

"Bon jour, madame," he said to Elida as soon as he met her eyes.

"Good morning, friend," he said to Phillip.

He approached Emma, blessing her with the amulets he was holding, then gave them a big hug and invited them in so they could rest a bit from the trip, and from the sorrows of having to run away all the time to save their lives.

It did not seem strange to Phillip that that man knew the reasons why they had come to that place so far from their home.

He knew that at some point someone suitable would appear to help them continue on their way towards the north, but he did not remember having had any vision of that mysterious man, who offered them the help they needed at that moment. Like Elida, his intuition made him think that at least they had a chance to rest.

They stayed for a few days at Low Burnett's house, while they decided what to do because they were not sure whether to stay in that place or continue further north. Phillip and Elida had to take many things into account before deciding to continue because they could not allow any of the villains who were chasing them to harm them. Much less hurt little Emma, who was innocent of the petty greed of these manipulators of the truth, and who control the world with their lies.

That same night Low invited them to a rite that he had prepared especially for them, so that they would not run into any risks, since the rite was with the sole intention of helping them, because God wanted it that way and because that was his obligation; Furthermore, he told them that it was essential that Emma receives the requisite blessings that she would need in retaking her kingdom.

Elida turned to see Phillip somewhat disturbed by what Low had said, but Phillip took her hand and smiled at her, looking straight into her eyes.

At that moment, Elida could hear Phillip tell her that everything would be fine and that she should not worry. She got a little dizzy from the impression she had from having heard Phillip inside her head, without him moving his lips, because it was something she had never experienced.

"How is it possible?" Elida thought, in the midst of the confusion, a reason formed in her mind.

Low put his hand on Elida's forehead, so Elida began to have visions of a distant future, where she watched her daughter cry in anguish and suffering, without her being able to help her in any way.

Phillip knew that this was necessary for Elida on her spiritual path because that was her moment; just as it was for him in the pyramid of The Old Lady with the White Hair.

Without intervening, he just stared with great attention to not miss any details, and to learn more about his own path; Well, perhaps, one day he would have to do the same when the time comes, or when he understands the necessary lessons while obtaining the gift of guiding others on their spiritual path. Elida came back from her trance with an immense desire to cry, to the point of not being able to stand, so she fell to her knees in front of Low. He extended his hand to Phillip as a sign that everything was fine and told him to wait for her to get back up on her own, that this was necessary for her initiation.

Elida got up after a couple of minutes, when she had already assimilated what was happening inside her being, still with some questions about the nature of what had happened to her; Well, she wanted to find an answer within the logic of thought that would clear up the confusion that she still felt a little. After a few minutes, and some answers from Low and Phillip, Elida had clarity in her being regarding her own experience in her life, being able to understand the reason why she had reincarnated this time. The details about some events that she had seen in her visions were not very clear to her, but she knew that in time everything would be revealed to her.

"La révélation ignites a certain temp, madame," Low Burnett said to Elida.

"Oui c'est le cas," Elida replied, looking into his eyes.

Elida put Emma one of the dresses that she had made together with her grandmother and her good friend Mama Chayo, for the rite that would take place at three in the morning in a small cave that was near that region.

Phillip took the Book of Raziel with him in his backpack, because he felt that he would need it at some point.

Outside the grotto were twelve monks, who were waiting for them with flowers and incense. All dressed in black with gold belts. Six young women dressed in white sprinkled rose petals on the nine steps, which they had to go down to reach the altar for the rite.

Low took Emma by the hand and led her to the altar, where there was a throne carved in stone, and adorned with precious stones, while Elida and Phillip stayed in front of the altar, along with other strange characters unknown to them. And who also seemed very different from anyone else; even so, they remained firm before the importance of what was happening with their daughter, because they recognized in their hearts that all this was inevitable. That the only thing they could do was support their daughter on her way to her destiny.

Phillip noticed the blue stone that was under the throne, from which a faint ultraviolet light began to emanate, which made him feel as if his spirit wanted to leave his body.

Elida held his hand strongly, and he felt how her spirit touched him; Well, he could even see how they touched each other beyond the bones and aching flesh. He tried to pay attention to everything that was happening in case he was having a vision or a dream regarding the situation. Because of the peculiarity of what was happening, made him think that was not real, despite having had enough experience to know the difference.

Behind the altar, which had a rose quartz wall, four people came out. The highest imam of faith and love, next to the heir to the lineage of God's people, to the right of the altar.

A royal knight, who wore a silver chain with a gold cross around his neck, came out from the same side, together with a woman dressed in a white cloak, which shed a golden light all around, with a crown so bright on her head, that you could hardly see her face. Unless you paid enough attention, and the view adjusted to the intensity of light that the woman radiated.

They stood next to the altar and raised their hands to heaven pronouncing some words in a language that neither Phillip nor Elida knew, nor had ever heard. Then, all at the same time said: «Praise Emma, so that your intention of love and justice is released in your awakening».

Phillip and Elida did not let go of the link that united their spirits, and they felt like they were floating in the air, because the ultraviolet light sustained them. They could see their bodies below them, just like everyone else's, except for

Emma, who glowed sitting on the throne in body and spirit at the same time.

Suddenly they all returned to their bodies, at the moment when the woman dressed in light tried to speak to Emma in her ear.

The royal knight hurried to where the woman of light was and insisted that it was not the right time for men to know that part of the truth. That she should consider the master's plan and vision, before letting the men take care of that part.

The heir to the lineage of the people of God advised that the signs had not yet been given, so the law should be respected at all times, to not fall into any fault that would spoil what was designated from on high. While everyone was silent about what was happening, Emma's sweet and innocent voice was heard saying:

"Sanity and reason." With that characteristic voice of babies like when they are learning to speak and they do not pronounce some letters of the words, but enough so that everyone perfectly understands the intention.

The Imam cordially approached them to offer his help, telling them that the law of the spirit guaranteed men; Well, they were these spirits too. He kindly asked them, as brothers in creation, to consider each other, and to consider man as well.

"There must be no division in purpose," said the Imam, "nor resistance to the law of the creator."

An old man came out of the rose quartz wall carrying a spear in his hand, which he used as a walking stick to support himself when walking.

The four prostrated themselves before him as a sign of respect for his hierarchy. He stood in front of Emma and pointed his spear just above her forehead, just as the blue stone radiated the ultraviolet light most intensely.

"The plan is still in motion, and so is the intention." The old man said while he looked at the four prostrated on the right side of the altar. He turned around and stared into Phillip's eyes, at the moment when he pointed the spear right at his heart, and said, "Your part will be, it will be in your hands."

The old man left the same way he had come through the rose quartz wall, then the four of them stood up, each leaning close to Moonlight to whisper in her ear.

The woman of light gave her a cane carved from an olive branch, with a crystal at the tip, so that she would direct the light of sanity to men, and the brightness of understanding to achieve recognition of themselves.

The royal knight gave her a silver chain with a gold talisman, which was carved with holy signs. So that, at the right time, she could claim her right in the world, to reign with the truth of love and justice.

The heir to the lineage of God's people and highest rabbi approached her and anointed Emma's head with olive oil and gave her a small Smyrna plant in a glass container, to protect her from being poisoned by the vanity or greed of the material world.

The highest Imam of faith and love approached her offering his humble service as a spiritual guide, advising Emma about the misunderstandings that she would possibly come across on her way, and which are the same ones we all have in carnal life.

He told her that every human being had the right to know the truth of universal love. Of that mantra that vibrates in the melody of love, which creates at the same time everything that is and what is not.

The Imam made a bow of humility before Emma approached her taking from his turban the papyrus of the law, which he gave to Emma so that she would be prudent when considering her own ideas; Well, he warned her that her confusion would assail her at a certain moment, like pride or fear, but that she should be prudent. Above all, in the decisions that she came to make, so that she would not misunderstand herself at the moment of believing that she is doing the right thing.

The Imam swore to help her retake the leadership of sanity and peace in the world, with solidarity brotherhood, without distinctions of creeds or confused fanaticisms, worked by ignorance of intentions.

He also gave her three honey-colored dates, which seemed to shine by themselves, so that she would resist her body until the last moment of the battle, which would be the beginning of her victory.

Elida and Phillip were surprised at how these characters spoke to Emma, as if she were an older person who understood all those sublime details. But each one of them understood within their being, that Moonlight understood with her spirit everything that they said to her, at the moment of seeing her approve with her head what the four offered her with their advice, and of hearing her speak coherently with the others four on some details of their advice.

The Imam called Phillip to come to the altar, so Elida let go of his hand so that he could go where he was called. Phillip stood in front of the Imam, and said:

"Tell me, what good is my humble presence to you?"

"The book and the key, Phillip," the Imam told him, and held out his hand, so Phillip had no hesitation and took it out of the bag to hand it over.

The Imam showed the book to the woman of light, who placed her hand on it and the book opened to the indicated page; then the Imam handed it over to Philip to read.

Phillip took the book, a little unsure of being able to read what it said, because he did not know what language it was written in.

"Every spirit recognizes its language." The Imam told him.

The blue stone irradiated ultraviolet light more intensely, at the moment when Phillip began to recite the words of the book.

The message was on a spiritual level, since all those present were transformed into spirits by the ultraviolet light, leaving their physical bodies next to them, to listen to the words that sealed the agreement between heaven and earth.

The woman of light called Elida to come closer as well. Elida immediately went to be in front of her, extended her hand and the woman of light responded to her greeting.

Elida realized that she was in her spirit, for she had left her body behind her the moment she had been called. The woman of light touched Elida's chest, and a white light came out illuminating the entire place. «The agreement is made; the truth will come. Now you can do your part in the plan », the woman of light told Elida, so Elida returned to her place with a great feeling of happiness. Phillip took the book and returned to his place next to Elida, at the moment when the four characters left through the rose quartz wall.

_jema_sid

Chapter 6
The Crown Of Justice

Holding hands, Elida and Phillip opened their eyes to see that the altar had disappeared, along with everything else that was inside the cave, leaving only the stone where Emma lay sleeping, and some things that Low had for the rites. They were sitting on the ground, each holding a bowl with a concoction Low had given them.

"Everything is real, but not of this world, buddy." Low told Phillip, at the moment when Phillip turned to see him standing next to the stone where Emma was lying.

"Vous pou vez l'emmener au lit, madame." Low told Elida.

Elida was a bit confused to see that they were the only ones in the cave. She could not explain what had happened. Although she suspected what it was about, she did not dare to say a single word. She knew that everything was possible, so she did not doubt the symbology of all that, nor the responsibility that represented for her or for her beloved daughter.

She took Emma and led her to a small room outside the small grotto, where they had already prepared a place for her to lie down. Two of Low's assistants settled her in her bed along with Elida so that she could rest a bit since it was almost dawn.

Phillip had stayed talking to Low for a while longer because Low had asked him to.

He told Phillip that a new lesson in his life was necessary for him to continue on his way; In addition, he told him that he already had everything resolved so that at dawn they would leave for Palacios, where they would board Captain J. Cousteau's ship. To then sail along the coast of the gulf until arriving at Marsh Island.

As soon as the sun came up, Low offered them something to eat, as well as telling them that they should get out as soon as possible, because the ship would leave in a couple of hours. That the captain was already aware and agreed to take them, so there was no time to waste.

Low gave Phillip a message on a papyrus to deliver to the person he had indicated, at the time he needed. And he insisted that he should not fear what fate had in store for him, what he could not specify in his visions or in his dreams.

Phillip took the papyrus and put it in the bag where he kept the book, he thanked Low for what he had done for them and promised his friendship despite the distance.

"Thank you, night." Phillip told him, at the moment they left the town behind.

Low Burnett, who was about thirty-three years old, knew a lot of people of different nationalities, from the work he did trading rare items and magic potions, and he was also a very good friend of Captain Cousteau.

In Palacios, Low gave the captain a big hug when boarding the ship, to which the captain responded with the same impetus of joy, for being able to see each other again after a few years.

He introduced them to Captain Cousteau, who was decent in receiving them.

After agreeing on the basics, Low and the captain gloated a bit on the deck of the ship, while the boatswain and two biology students helped Elida and Emma with the things they brought, to carry them to a cabin that they had set up especially for them. Phillip went with the boatswain to tell him how he could be useful, because he would not allow him to tell him that he could not do anything. The boatswain looked at him very serenely for a few seconds and told him that bragging was not allowed on the ship, nor were liars allowed, much less thieves. That he better stop talking, because he should be helping the two young men who were trying to fit some boxes on the deck at that moment. Phillip approved what the boatswain had said, leaving immediately to help those intrepid young men in whatever was necessary. They received him with sympathy and happy to be able to count with his help.

He took on the task of accommodating everything so that they could leave as quickly as possible. Faithfully believing as always that anything he did could have a positive influence. Common sense encouraged him to join in the task of casting off to leave the port and getting ready to navigate for a few hours, until they reached the point where the captain had predestined to stop to carry out an underwater exploration. That was what the two young men he was helping told him would happen, which would perhaps last until dawn the next day, if they were able to obtain the necessary information to fulfill the plan estimated in the captain's logbook in the indicated time.

Phillip enjoyed the following hours of sailing learning everything that the young people told him about the flora and fauna that existed in the sea, the endless adventures with Captain Cousteau, and exploring new places each time to discover the beauty of our planet. Phillip told them what he had learned about some species that lived in the sea, thanks to some magazines from the National Geographic Society that he had found in the garbage; In addition, he told them about some experiences he had as a collector when he lived in the dump.

The youngsters were amazed to hear Phillip talk about some plants that grew in that part of the gulf, which were related to the legend of the fountain of eternal youth.

They were men of scientific methods, not of legends or myths, but even so, they were impressed by Phillip's knowledge of these plants; details about their chemical composition, morphology, and the region where they grew. One of the young biologists, gaining confidence with Phillip, said that the captain's crazy things about some legends were the real reasons why he had formed his expedition, but that an investigative foray was necessary to cover up his plan.

Phillip did not give it too much importance, because of the way the young man had said it, because he was just being somewhat ironic, joking with the captain's personal tastes.

He told him that the captain would be interested in hearing about that tale of the fountain of youth and its mysterious plants.

The two young men laughed at the same time without any malice, but upholding the ethics regarding their methods, without even accepting to consider the issue.

Phillip realized that the young people were somewhat inflexible in their ideas and concepts, understanding that the rigidity of the methods had limited them to concrete answers, to concepts and ideas that other men reasoned before them.

He did not insist more on the plants but on sympathy and the willingness to learn something new.

He said goodbye to them saying that he had something to ask the captain about the trip, so the two young men laughed a little, thinking that Phillip would go and tell the captain about his fable. He did not give much importance to the disbelief of those young scientists and immediately left to try to talk to the captain.

The captain and the boatswain were in the cabin, looking at a map on the desk, at the moment when Phillip knocked on the door three times.

The boatswain opened the door saying very forcefully that he had asked that no one should bother them, to tell him immediately what they wanted. Phillip asked him to speak to the captain for a minute to ask him a few things, above all, the duration of the trip and the cost of taking them. The captain heard what Phillip was saying, so he asked the boatswain to let him in. Phillip introduced himself to the captain again, then asked him the same question about the cost of the trip and food for his family.

The captain looked him straight in the eye for a few seconds and then told him that it would not cost him a penny because his great friend Low had already repaid him with endless favors, and that he was doing it because of the great friendship they had. Phillip thanked him for his nobility, and offered his service in any way possible, to not be a burden in vain, insisting that he would help him in whatever he wanted.

Phillip looked at the map that was on top of the desk for a couple of seconds before the captain pulled it up and quickly rolled it up so he would not see what it was about.

The captain realized that Phillip had been staring lost in some memory of the past, instantly sensing that Phillip had some information related to that map. The boatswain walked towards Phillip to touch his shoulder and shook him a little to get him to react, but the captain held out his hand for him to stop. Phillip remembered those childhood afternoons when his father used to show him the things he kept in his old trunk, and he remembered that among those relics there was a map that was hidden in the trunk lid, very similar to the one the captain had in his possession.

The captain, seeing that Phillip was gaining some lucidity, asked him if he had seen a similar map in his life, that any clue would be of great help. Phillip told him that his trip would be in vain if he did not do the right thing with the plants and the crown of justice. The captain was scared listening to what Phillip was saying, because he knew what he was talking about, and he knew that hardly anyone in the world knew about such things; for which, he asked the bosun to leave immediately, to close the door and stay outside so that he would not allow anyone to interrupt them for any reason. The captain explained that each of the eight maps that had been found contained only clues about that mysterious island; just some clues about where to go but nothing related to the treasure. Phillip answered him very serenely explaining the reason why our ancestors had done it that way, precisely so that no one could ever know about those things; Well, men are very subtly corrupted by the comforts that power offers them. He insisted that men were not prepared to know that kind of truth. That it was not necessary to look for anything anywhere, because nowhere will give you what you already have.

The captain begged him to tell him more about the map, because that map was proof of the existence of objects made by those who lived before the deluge. That it was very important for humanity to know what they did wrong; and that way, we would try better this time.

Phillip was somewhat insecure about showing him the way to read the map in order to reach that mysterious island. He was also not sure if the captain was someone to trust, although he felt that he was not at risk. After thinking about it very well for a few seconds, he decided to share some things that could help him in his own path and understanding.

Captain J. Cousteau had never imagined that one day he would meet a person like Phillip, enlightened by the awakening of his spiritual being, and graced with the weight of protecting the truth.

He approached Phillip and made him a respectful bow, then very cordially told him that he was very grateful for letting him listen to his words, because he felt very fulfilled knowing the details that he had told him about the maps and their mystery. Phillip saw that the captain was pleased with what he had told him about The Tools of Order, and the reasons why they should not be within the reach of men. At the same time, he thought that he was making a mistake by telling him about these things, because it would encourage him more to search, instead of giving up looking for something new.

Confusion invaded him a little as he did not know what to do, because at that moment he felt a strange sensation in his throat that prevented him from saying anything. So, he took that as a sign so he would not tell him more than he should. It was too dangerous for him to know certain details, and he did not want the captain's life in danger by telling him some things he should not know.

In any case, he knew that the captain would not give up on his personal search, since it was clear that it had become the totality of his daily life, and he would never stop until he found the objects that fascinated his mind.

Phillip remembered the woman of light, when she said that every man had the right to know his truth and recognized within himself that this right belonged to the captain, in the same way as to every conscious being in creation; that, as such, he would tell him enough so that he himself could decide between what he should do and what was not correct to persist with.

Phillip asked the captain to come closer, put his hand into his backpack to touch the book, and said, "Shalom."

The captain fell to his knees as he saw a white light illuminate Phillip's head. He was amazed at what he saw, to such a degree that he was about to cry.

Phillip touched J. Cousteau's forehead with his other hand, while he continued touching the book inside his backpack. Suddenly, remembering all the good and bad things he had done in his life, the captain had a vision of a place that he sensed was not far from where they were at that moment, feeling the temptation to run away to correct the course.

But at the same time, he felt a sublime melancholy that saddened him greatly; Well, in his visions he could see men perfecting the technique of annihilating each other, in the fastest and most effective way, with all that creativity that their ambition for power generates.

His heart told him that whatever he came to find in his adventure for knowledge, he should keep quiet so as not to feed the ego that was taking over him at that moment; because in the same way, the men drowned in the waves of the ego would be tempted by the power that The Tools of Order cause their possessor, and they would try to kill their neighbor for the simple fact of not agreeing on the ideas that govern their world.

When he woke up from his vision, the captain was lying on the ground and with his eyes full of tears due to the sadness he felt when he saw the indifference that men come to have in themselves.

He stood up slowly without turning to see Phillip, because of the shame he felt knowing that Phillip was right, when he said that men were not prepared to face certain things of the truth. With sorrow on his face, he said, "Mon seigneur, je vous demande pardon." Captain J. Cousteau told him, "Mon obligation sera de protéger la vérité uniquement."

Phillip stared at him without saying a word, he just wondered the purpose that the divines had for all this, he also had a feeling that something would show up at the right time to give him the necessary clue, and know what to do, or where to go.

He told the captain that it was best to do the right thing, but he was still not sure he knew what was the right thing to do and what not to do. The captain told him that he would trust him, that he had command of his ship to direct it where he thought it wise to go. Phillip asked him to hold out the map to show him the correct way to read it.

Despite the fact that the captain was a sailor with many decades of experience, he did not object in the least, so he immediately took out the map so that Phillip could take a look at it. With the compass and the square, Phillip was able

114

to show the captain the exact place where they should find what he wanted so much. For Phillip it would be the perfect moment to face the mystery of the crown of justice and its power, which would help him to differentiate the practical from the ineffective, the reasonable from the irrational, and the just from the truth.

The captain was about to start a necessary path for his spirit, upon discovering the secrets that his heart longed for, and feeling part of those mysteries, having been initiated by Phillip with the gift of vision.

After a few minutes of Phillip explaining some details about his obligation as an initiate, the captain immediately went to change the navigation course towards that mysterious place, which was not supposed to exist, but which they would go in search of.

He did not tell the navigation officer who was in charge of the rudder about his intention to change the course, because he would surely tell the other scientists about what he had decided to do, and they would surely interrogate him demanding the reason why he had decided to do such a thing, without first consulting with them. The officer at the helm did not know the coordinates that the captain gave him, when ordering him to change course, that all he did was turn to look at him a little disconcerted, as if asking what was happening. The captain did not even turn to look at him, he just stared at the horizon through the cabin window, with a big smile that almost split his face in two.

Phillip returned to his cabin to see that his loved ones were okay, because he had been away for a couple of hours to go help the others. He told Elida what had happened with the scientists, when he helped them put some boxes on the deck, and what had happened with the captain in his cabin, while he carried Emma in her arms, since the little girl had thrown herself on top of him for the joy of seeing him arrive. Elida looked at him attentively while he talked without stopping about what had happened to him, but inside she felt an anguish that bothered her in her womb, for reasons that she had yet to discover. She interrupted him by giving him a kiss on the mouth, because she thought that this was the only way she would get him to stop talking, and also because she missed him a lot.

Elida asked him to stay with them for a while, to just hug them, that he did not have to say a single word, just be with them hugging them.

"Only while the sun goes down." Elida told him.

Phillip understood what Elida felt, so he hugged them tightly against his chest, while they watched the sunset together through the cabin window.

For the captain it was somewhat difficult to convince the scientists on board that the place where they would go would be very interesting for their research. That the flora and fauna of that island would be of great astonishment to them, well he insisted that he had already been to that place when he was a child. He told them that his grandfather had once taken him and his younger sister in his old Dutch ship, to this place that had been unexplored until then.

The biologists were a little interested, but they feared that it was one of the crazy things that the captain was already familiar with, so it would be a waste of time to look for a place that no one had ever heard of; Besides, the course to which they would go to study marine life had already been marked on the navigation charts. That, it would be unprofessional to search for myths or legends because they would risk of losing their reputation before the scientific society. At the end of their meeting, they all accepted the captain's decision, somewhat uneasy at not knowing where they were going, talking among themselves about some things that they did not agree on, but also hoping that something good would come out of all of this. Everyone minded their own business to not inquire too much into the captain's follies. Although they did not agree, they knew that they did not have much to do in the face of the enthusiasm that they already knew about him.

During the days of the trip, Phillip and Elida took advantage of every opportunity they could to show Emma the beauty of the sea, the life of a sailor and the adventures of those who try to be free; walking the ship from stern to bow to show her the people who were involved in the expedition.

Everyone adored that beautiful little girl, who gave each of them jasmine flowers when she saw them, and a kiss on their cheek so that they would go well in their search. According to the broken words of that beautiful princess.

Three days into the voyage, the captain and Phillip saw a large indigo sphere coming out of the deep waters of the gulf, when they were at the stern of the ship talking about the things that should be left behind, by continue on the path of the chosen to protect the truth.

Phillip felt his hair stand on end when he saw that unknown thing come out of the water, because he had never seen anything like it in his life, which was bigger than a bullring.

After marveling at the unusualness of that thing that seemed out of this world, the captain told him that on a couple of occasions he had seen something similar in those waters of the gulf, and that he was sure they had something to do with the crown of justice and its mystical power.

Phillip asked him to consider that many of the things are symbolic, and are not based on material objects, since these objects are only symbols of the potential that resides within all conscious beings.

The captain understood from his own experience what Phillip was referring to. At that moment, Phillip knew that everything was possible, that the truth was absolute and irremediable, regardless of the limitations that the perception of this reality creates in men, nor the discrepancies in their ideas. The occasion was so ephemeral that they were not able to alert the others so that they could see for themselves that marvel, which did not seem to have been invented by men. They stayed talking for a long time about the possibilities of what they had seen, unable to deny in any way what had really happened.

The captain told Phillip that he understood somehow that he had to keep quiet about some things to not be judged crazy, because he understood that everyone would have to experience it for themselves to understand or believe the wonders of creation.

Phillip looked at him with pleasure, realizing that he had chosen well, starting him on his own search for the truth. He placed his hand on his heart, telling him that the duty of every being man or woman, was to be free to understand the reason why they exist. Phillip tried to reason what the captain argued about the right to know the purpose that the divine put in our lives. The captain said that some powerful people took advantage of the naivety of the ill-educated, favoring the greed that devours their hearts, with pleasures that only the flesh takes advantage of, but in doing so their spirits lost the unique opportunity of the moment.

"No earthly or foreign being, aware of life, should take advantage of the weak and ignorant, or oppose the final purpose of our creator," Phillip told him.

"Précisément monseigneur," replied the captain.

On the sixth day they reached the island which was not supposed to exist on any conventional map, and which had only been visited by very few who were graced with the invitation so that their bodies could walk on the land, which was full of all kinds of fruits and extravagant fauna. One of the biologists was the one who watched it rise from the ocean waters, with the first rays of the sun behind the island, giving it the marvelous color of its coast, as well as its geographical extension, which was located in the middle of where the

118

ocean current ascended, where a wall of water was formed that prevented it from being seen by any ship that passed through that latitude. It was that same current that took them to the island, thanks to a maneuver that Phillip showed the captain, when they reached the point where the current emerged, because it was necessary to position the ship in such a way that the current would take it to the west side of the island, where the only access to enter was.

Everyone in the bows watched as they collided with something that looked like a giant wave but had a low slope in relation to the height seen at some distance, and a thickness on the surface of the emerging current, of a couple of leagues, and which descended until it reached a lower current that surrounded the island. The captain admired with great respect the maneuver that Phillip had made to get into the nearest current, the same one that later dragged them to the stone pier where they got stuck.

The black marble pier seemed to have been made by people who apparently inhabited the island. There was a white marble corridor inlaid with rubies and emeralds, which apparently served as a way for people to move orderly around the pier.

The ship's cargo door was right in a corridor that was made of a different type of stone, perhaps for heavier loads.

The pier seemed to accommodate three ships of the same size as Captain J. Cousteau's.

Next to the pier, towards the east side of the island, there was a type of mechanism that apparently served to lift loads to a different height, to then transport them to the interior of the island by a rope mechanism, which from that distance seemed of gold.

All the scientists on the ship were anxious to get down, and to be able to take a look at all the wonder that was glimpsed on all sides. The astonishment was exaggerated on their faces, almost to the point of crying. One of them almost jumped overboard, because of the ecstasy he felt at being in that place, which was not supposed to exist, but shone before his eyes like a great jewel full of sublime light, or like a paradise full of ambrosia.

The boatswain and two other members of the crew prevented that poor botanist from jumping to certain death in time, for he was bewitched by the wonders he beheld everywhere.

Suddenly he went into a nervous breakdown, which caused him great anxiety, so he began to writhe and cry inconsolably. He yelled at them for mercy to let him go, because he felt that he was dead and that this place was paradise.

The captain and Phillip immediately went down to attend the poor man, who did not stop crying inconsolably, insisting over and over again that they let him jump to paradise; and endless more inconsistencies that reason attempted in his lost mind. Phillip approached him, took him by the hand, and said:

"Your mind must be serene, your heart clean and your spirit ready for the truth. Give up the old and accept the new."

That young botanist named Carlos Darwin insisted that none of this was logical or natural, that perhaps he was hallucinating or dreaming; for which he asked one of his fellow explorers to pinch him to make sure it was not a dream. The young entomologist replied that it was not a dream at all, and immediately helped Phillip lift Carlos so that he could see for the second time and with his own eyes, that inexplicable paradise in the middle of the ocean.

It did not seem that they would convince him not to jump, because he was truly ready to surrender to that sublime paradise that enchanted him with its almost unreal light. In the same way, some others were unable to believe what they could not deny it anymore, so they had to swallow their pride.

It took time for many to accept that this place was real, because it did not seem to be known by any science, nor was there any record of exploration by any society.

After a while the captain and Phillip tried to clarify some things with the crew and the scientists, Elida left the cabin carrying Emma in her arms. She walked a bit towards where the others were, but she stopped because at that moment a strange breeze fluttered around the two of them, as if an inexplicable call caught her attention, right towards where the side loading door of the ship was.

On the path there was a glimpse of a figure that seemed to be a very tall and thin person, with reddish skin; with long hair blacker than night; with a plume of quetzal feathers on his head.

Phillip turned to see Elida when he heard her speak with a fixed look towards the landing path, where this peculiar being with a simple appearance was, similar in size to the same being that he had seen in the chapel of Father Joaquín, when they had to flee through the tunnel that was under the chapel.

He kept thinking about the reason why he had not heard anything, since the call was not for him this time, and it felt a little strange to see that his loved ones were called by that being.

"The honor is ours, Chilam Balam." Elida murmured, staring at the being.

Suddenly, Phillip heard inside his head an overwhelmingly sweet and convincing voice, which told him that only the two of them could get off the ship, that those who were predestined to receive what the agreement of the divine demanded, each would have their turn at the time indicated by him; furthermore, that it was necessary that no one should go down without being allowed to do so.

Phillip turned to see the captain to try to tell him what he had heard, but the captain replied that he knew what that being had said. That he should not worry that he could accompany Elida and Emma to the ship's side unloading door., while he stayed behind to explain to the scientists what was going on.

Phillip stayed inside the boat while Elida and Emma walked to where this being was, who made a respectful bow to them at the moment they appeared before him. Two beings appeared behind the spiritual master, bringing with them a small trunk, from which they took out a silver-colored crown, with precious stones embedded within the sacred signs with which it had been carved.

The Chilam Balam gave it to Emma as a sign of celestial hierarchy, so that she would reign with the justice of truth, and not the ignorance with which men tend to lose the notion of their being.

Phillip had listened to everything that the master had told Emma, for which reason he felt a great pain in his abdomen at the thought that one day he could lose her, having to face the vicissitudes that life brings, in the lessons that are generously given to us among the details that we commonly ignore.

Elida tucked the crown into little Moonlight's dress, which lit up as if it were a sea of stars covering her, silvery moonlight beneath her feet, and the sun shining behind her. Making Phillip fall to his knees, and clasping his hands against his chest, with the certainty that he would lose her one day, when she would have to fly with her own wings.

"Get up Phillip, for the master is not bigger than his servant, nor is the servant bigger than him; Well, only The Creator is worthy and fair of admiration. Your part will come, be prudent."

Phillip had heard inside his head what that being was telling him, so he got up to receive Elida and Emma, because at that moment they were returning to the cargo hold of the ship. He noticed that Elida was crying, perhaps because she knew like him, that children must fly by themselves at some

122

point in their lives; so that, like themselves, they find the reason why they exist.

The master asked Phillip to come closer to him, so Phillip walked towards him, still with tears on his face due to the melancholy he felt, as he sensed the possible future of his beloved daughter. The master asked him not to fear the uncertainty that his mortal reason caused in his spirit, which should be firm in his convictions, about what he should do to achieve the purpose that the divine had planned in him.

"The Book, Phillip." The master asked.

Phillip took it out of his backpack and handed it over to one of the beings, who took it to the master and handed it over to him.

The Chilam Balam opened the book to a specific page by passing his other hand over it. He uttered the sacred words that vibrate in nothingness, which it sustains us as alive on all spiritual levels. And he told him that this meeting had been made to attest to his part in the melody, as to what the divines had entrusted to him, that now it was his turn to face reason before he ventured into awakening.

The master returned the book to Phillip with his own hand, at the same moment that he touched it on the forehead with the index finger of his left hand.

Phillip had a vision of a world where there were plants and minerals full of light, which fed the beings that lived in that place. And who also had a very long life, thanks to the food that that beautiful paradise provided them. The vision did not show him that he was in that world, he could only see him from afar, in a place that felt like he was floating on a giant rock in space, next to other beings that supported him in his mission.

As soon as the master removed the finger from Phillip's forehead, he came to his senses and immediately took the book to put it in his backpack, at the moment the master told him that the key was in his heart. The master promised three visits to the island for everyone on the ship, but that this time they should leave as soon as possible, because it was not wise to stay long on the island at that time; Well, the insatiable indifference of the serpent is lurking at all times, and he defined to them that in due course they would receive the invitation so that they could return.

Many cried, but Phillip consoled them saying that the promise was made, so that each one would have their share at the right time to attend the call, that their spirit should not fail.

They left that paradise with the hope of one day being able to return to enjoy its ambrosia and its spiritual wisdom. They all resigned their hope to the promise, but they cemented their faith by having witnessed a part of the absolute truth. No one could ever again deny the mysterious and unknown path that the divine use to guide the chosen ones, not only where they must go, but also what they must do at a certain moment, in order to know the truth about life.

In a few more days after leaving the island, they arrived at Marsh Island, where with the help of a friend of the captain, Phillip and his family were taken in a smaller boat to the yellow bayou; then, to the Atchafalaya River to continue their journey towards the north.

Chapter 7
Hopeless Faith

After navigating the Atchafalaya River for a few hours, they reached a place where they disembarked to spend the night. A lady was waiting for them at the river dock with flowers and incense burning in golden bowls.

Two more people who came with the lady helped with the suitcases to take them to a cabin that was in the middle of the swamp.

Despite being complete strangers, they were received and treated with great care and respect. In the same way, Elida and Phillip wholeheartedly appreciated the great detail of offering them their house to be able to rest.

They avoided excessive formalities to make the most of the opportunity to relax from the trip, and so that little Moonlight could get some sleep.

Without any news, that was one of those rare nights where they did not have much to deal with, so after some time they slept properly without fear.

The next morning, the lady named Asia Rothschild offered them to eat some roasted crocodile, mixed with magical plants, which grew on that side of the swamp. And some tea for the stress that the trip may have caused them. They both drank tea with the conviction that the lady was absolutely correct in asking about the tension that was almost killing them. It was evident that they needed it because they both broke their sentence to ask him for some more of that delicious magical tea.

Elida did not eat meat because she was a vegetarian, but Phillip and Emma ate some of the crocodile meat because they were hungry; furthermore, the smell that the plants gave it was almost irresistible to the human palate.

Mrs. Asia offered Elida some fruits in a silver bowl that seemed to shine on their own, as well as a glass of wine that radiated a very dim violet light.

Nothing was strange for anyone anymore, especially for little Emma, who grew up experiencing everything that happened in the path of her parents, who tried to show her as much as they could in life, so that she learned all that as something intimate and natural.

"The note, Phillip." Mrs. Rothschild told him.

Phillip was convinced that she was the right person, because of the feeling he felt in his chest at the moment when Mrs. Asia extended her hand to him to give it to her. Phillip took it out of the backpack and handed it to the lady, thinking that she would have something to do with getting them on the right path to continue their journey.

They stayed in the swamp for a few days, until the right moment for the moon to appear at the correct coordinates on the horizon, to carry out the necessary rite so that they could continue safely to the next place, where they would have to deal with what divine providence had planned for them from the highest spheres of spiritual evolution.

As a sign of gratitude for hosting them in her cabin, Phillip helped Mrs. Asia's eldest son in the garden that they had around the cabin, which served as a barrier to prevent any strange animal or evil spirit from entering and trying to harm them. The young man introduced himself to Phillip after he left the cabin to take a look around.

Phillip was struck by the layout of the garden and the plants that grew in that fertile and almost magical land, where there were some of the same species of plants that his father had planted in the garden of the hats where they lived, which his mother taught him to take care and reap its fruits. That caused him a melancholic smile when he remembered those eternal afternoons in which he boasted of learning from his mother's advice. He could feel her presence in the butterflies that flew around him, in the soft and subtle way of the wind touching his skin, and in the sublime magic of the scene. He was about to tear up when he almost smelled her aroma, which was hidden among the flowers.

A moss path was illuminated a little by the sunlight coming out from between the clouds, making Phillip feel confident to walk where the path led him, because of the call he felt in his heart, suggesting that he should go to that place.; which he found not far from the cabin in a small clearing full of flowers that opened up among the swamp.

"Nor Rood," the young man told him.

"Philip," he answered.

They talked for a long time while they worked with the flowers, which grew only in that little wasteland of the swamp and moved the earth and relocated some plants in different places to protect the flowers from voracious insect pests.

Phillip told him that he should go back to the cabin to bring his daughter and his wife to meet him, but Nor told him not to worry, that he would visit them in due time, because he had some work to do with the flowers before he can go back home. Phillip replied that it was fine, but if he needed his help, he would not hesitate to let him know.

Upon returning to the cabin, Elida and Emma were in the garden together with Mrs. Asia enjoying the peace that the place made them feel, because it felt as if time did not pass. Such a thing caught Phillip's attention, and when he understood it, he insisted to Mrs. Asia to help them leave as soon as possible, because he felt that if they neglected, they would stay in that place forever.

She replied that the time was near, that the night of the indicated day had come with the sun of that morning, that he should prepare to leave the following day for the owl ceremony. Near the ground where the flowers grew, there was an altar that resembled a giant stone owl, where thirty-three hooded men stood pronouncing an ancient creed to control the forces of nature.

Everyone was silent at the moment they arrived at the place, thanks to the fact that Mrs. Asia raised her cane and spoke a few words in the language that Phillip was already familiar with.

Neither Elida nor Phillip was allowed to reach the altar, only the girl had to approach a small rectangular stone that was at the feet of the great owl, on which Emma sat by herself and with a big smile on her face.

All those presents knelt before her at the moment when the little Moonlight raised her right hand pointing towards the sky. The grand master came out behind the owl with a crystal that did not reflect the light, nor the image of what was around it; he walked slowly over to Emma and handed it over. At that moment, the crystal shone with great intensity until the light turned dark as nothing, then everything lit up as if it were dawn and the first rays of the sun gave color to things.

"Justice must prevail not only with mortals." The grand master told little Moonlight.

The girl looked at him with great tenderness and raised her right hand to touch the forehead of the grand master, who leaned down so that little Emma could touch him. The grand master moved close to her as if to have Emma whisper something in his ear, then he left the same way he had come.

Mrs. Asia and her son Nor accompanied Emma from the altar, to where Elida and Phillip were holding hands, waiting for their daughter to return from her obligations as an independent being.

Walking back to the cabin, they came across the path that led to the small flower moor where Phillip had met Nor Rood. And at the suggestion of Mrs. Asia, they took the path to go to that place, where the light of the moon bathed the flowers with its magical glow. Suddenly the crystal began to shine inside Phillip's backpack, because he had kept it there when he took Emma in his arms, to leave that place where the stone owl was. The sacred signs of the book were illuminated with an intense gold that could be seen through Phillip's backpack.

An intense light that came down from the moon levitated the crown that was among Emma's dress, until it was positioned on top of the flowers and ascended until disappearing with the moonlight.

Phillip thought about the call for justice that he felt came from that mysterious place, which accompanied this planet in its harmonious dance of implicit complicity.

He felt that all this was a sign of destiny so that he would begin to recognize the importance of his mission in this carnal life.

Elida had Emma by the hand, while Phillip was a few steps in front of them, looking at the moon with anguish, not knowing how to attend to the call that his spirit felt.

He took his daughter and embraced her along with his beloved Elida, at the moment when Mrs. Asia told him that the reward of justice will be executed by those who understood the truth of universal love. Whether mortal or divine, the obligation of each being is that of justice and love. They both humbly accepted the advice that the holy woman gave them, and they promised to do with dignity as much as their strength and possibilities allowed them.

Without a doubt, they had a lot to talk about that night, which they did not waste to properly plan the next step.

At six-fifteen in the morning, they left to sail north on the Atchafalaya River, with a little more fear than usual, but with the hope that one day they would finally have a place to rest peacefully. For now, they just had to continue on their way. They reached the Red River without incident and were tucked in the tri-river area for a day before continuing north up the Mississippi.

They stayed in a small cabin that was next to the river, where they would spend the night and then continue their journey in the morning. After having made sure that his loved ones ate something, and that they were comfortable, Phillip went out for a while to see the stars.

When trying to discover the mystery of the night, Phillip heard the sad voice of a woman, which distressed him a little because of the pain that her pleas denoted. He immediately recognized the language that the woman spoke in the middle of the night, which was the same language from where he came from. He called her asking her what was wrong with her, but he did not receive an answer, he only listened to the moans and laments of the woman, crying out for mercy to let them go. The painful moan with which the woman tried to seek help in the darkness of nowhere was intriguing to Phillip, who immediately paid attention to where the moans were coming from. He fearlessly entered the forest guided by the anguished crying of the innocent being, despite not being able to see beyond his nose.

Not far from the river, there was a shed where the peasants kept their animals at night and kept machinery to work in the fields, where Phillip arrived following the complaints of that poor woman, who did not stop begging for mercy to let them go.

Arriving at the side of the galley, he looked through a hole in the old wall that was almost about to fall, as a tall man with a robust and savage appearance was beating a woman tied to a piece of wood that was lying on the floor. A middle-aged man was tied to a post with his mouth covered and showing signs of having been beaten; Well, one of his eyes had closed completely due to the bruise caused by the blows.

Phillip realized that the savage had a rifle near him, as well as a huge knife at his waist. He could not compete against him. He felt that if that man found out he would kill him without hesitation. He felt his heart break out from the pain, seeing so much injustice and wickedness, although he knew that this was the petty nature of deceived and ignorant men.

At the same time, he felt powerless before the imposition and power of that irrational creature who subjected the innocent to his ferocious shameful sadism.

He felt great fear because the situation was not in his hands, because he did not have the ability to save them from the abuser, who took advantage of their lives to quench his thirst for lust and racial hatred.

He thought about his family resting in the cabin next to the river, and how important it was to them because he could not leave them alone in that strange and unknown place. That for no reason could risk his life to save those people from their misfortune. And he thought that if that was the will of the creator, he had nothing to do about it.

He turned around to go back to the cabin, but at that moment he had a vision of himself crying out for mercy, in a terrifying place that caused excruciating pain throughout his body, which he saw was almost destroyed. The vision left when he heard the pleas of that poor woman again, so he immediately got up from where he had fallen at the moment of having the vision, to turn around, staring at the galley.

Because of that mystical force that keeps us firmly on the path, he took the courage that was born in his heart to face adversity without fear of losing his life.

He stared at that injustice between the unnailed boards of the walls, thanks to the light of the oil lamp that the man had hung on a pole, which had some mysterious signs marked all over it, which reminded Phillip of his path and the obligation that he had regarding divine justice, as well as love and mercy.

Convinced that he was not alone in his intention to help regardless of the risk of losing his life, he went to the galley thinking that the force of justice would help him face the villain, with the necessary arguments to make him understand the error in which he was missing his chance to know mercy. He walked determined and without doubting who he was and what he was capable of doing, as well as feeling the divine force in his intentions.

Upon reaching the door, Phillip extended his hand to open it, but it opened by itself before he touched it, due to a precise and almost lively wind, which whipped it strongly, making the whole place rumble.

"Enough!" Phillip yelled at him, "Stop your ignorance, you wretched cretin!"

That man with eyes bluer than the sky of the field, turned around when he felt the wind enter strongly at the moment when Phillip yelled at him to stop, quickly taking his gun, and aiming Phillip at the head. Phillip looked him firmly in the eyes without any fear of losing his life and convinced that justice would triumph at the end of all the misunderstandings, then he insisted that he give up his iniquity, and repent of his disrespect towards those whom he believed were weak and helpless.

That was one of those moments in which he regretted not having brought the medallion and the pectoral with him, knowing that no wicked would compete against it. Either way, he reached into his backpack to touch the book, which gave him the strength to continue without fear. He trusted that the divine would know what to do to protect them from the ignorance with which the unhappy man was deceived.

When it was obvious that that iniquitous ignorant would not give up his foolishness, for wasting his moment to learn better things for the spirit, the light of the oil lamp intensified greatly, drawing the attention of the abuser, who immediately turned to see because of how strange that light seemed to him; besides, the light seemed to pull the rifle just like his spirit out of the body. What frightened that unhappy fool in a great way was feeling how the light brought to his mind all the misdeeds he did as a child, all those things that he had learned from his parents and that he kept until they became his way of life. He was judged by his own conscience; how to escape it.

Taking advantage of the burning epiphany of that ignorant abuser, Phillip ran to take the lady's dress to cover her private parts while he untied her from the plank lying on the floor. He then untied that poor badly injured man to be able to give him some wine that he brought in his canteen, believing that with that he would at least keep him alive.

Trying to keep fear at bay, he hurried as fast as he could to help them, but without ceasing to keep an eye on the evil created by pride.

Turning to look at that ignorant man and abuser of innocents, Phillip could see that he was on his knees staring at the oil lamp, while the rifle had been left lying on the ground. Although it crossed his mind to take it and end the life of that haughty evildoer, Phillip preferred to save lives instead of taking them, remembering that this was precisely part of his mission in this life. He concentrated solely on finding a way out of that miserable place.

"Thanks, brother." That was the only thing that poor badly wounded man could say to Phillip, before losing consciousness due to his wounds.

The lady drew strength from where even she did not know she had, and together with Phillip, they lifted him up to flee from that place. Let us say that he was guided only with his heart because it was so dark that he could not see past his nose. When they arrived at the cabin, Elida was at the door looking towards the forest, waiting for Phillip to return, worried about the sensation she felt in her belly, which warned her that something was not right. She ran to help them just as the light from the oil lamp, which hung on a pole outside the cabin, illuminated them enough to see them in the dead of night. They entered the cabin immediately, but to their miserable luck, the owner of the boat was not around to help them get out of that place, because everyone's lives would be in danger if they stayed any longer. This caused the anguish of the lady, who did not stop insisting that they should leave as soon as possible. Elida tried to calm her down a bit while she watched Phillip deal with that poor badly injured man.

Phillip realized the anguish of the lady, who was absolutely right when she said that perhaps that miserable man would persecute them to kill them. He could not for any reason put the life of his family at risk.

After making sure that they were a little better, since their condition was heartbreaking and sad, Elida and Phillip talked about what they could do to try to save the lives of these poor people, considering the burden that meant what was happening to them.

It was not that they did not want to help them escape, what happened was that they did not want their lives to be at risk by being next to them; even so, they decided to flee on the ship as quickly as possible so that they could not be found.

Phillip took all the suitcases quickly to the ship, and some food for the road, while Elida was in charge of accommodating Emma in the cabin bed and then helping Phillip to get on board that poor dying man who seemed not to come to himself.

Somehow, Phillip managed to turn the boat on, and they got out of that place as fast as they could. More with divine help than anything else, for they could not see where they should go because of the darkness of the night.

They sailed up the Mississippi for a few hours before turning on any lights, first assuring themselves that the danger was past, so that another ship sailing up the river might see them, and they would not cause a collision or arouse some suspicion on the part of anyone who might realize that the ship was sailing without lights at night. Despite the fact that they did not see any sign of another ship or people who lived next to the river for many hours of navigation.

With the passage of time, trust grew once more in that poor lady, due to the heroic deed with which they had literally saved their lives. What she was going through was that she was trying to spit out of her that past that still hurt her every second and every breath she took.

The lady named Ruth de Chipilín, told Elida that she and her husband Seth Chipilín had arrived in the country a few years ago, with the hope of finding work and being able to seek a better future for the children they had left behind in their country of origin. She told her that they had worked in a hotel for a while, in a community that was close to the place where they later went to work, on the property of that unhappy abuser. He had promised them a place to sleep, and that he would pay them minimum wage to take care of the farm animals. That they did not even worry about food and other false promises. She told her that after arrived at that place, and after realizing the injustice he was committing to others that he had hidden in different galleys on his property, they tried to escape one night when the wretch tried to rape her for the first time. They went out through a hole in the galley, after having put the animals inside and making sure that the boss had gone to the big house.

Their surprise was that the indifferent abuser had more cronies under his command, who guarded the galleys so that no one tried to escape. They caught them trying to jump over the fence that divided the grazing field for the cattle, where they were beaten almost to death, and then they were taken on a couple of mules to the big house to expose them in front of the boss, who became very angry, that he nearly strangled Seth out of the anger he felt. Ruth realized that the wretch would kill him. She could not let that wretch get away with it for any reason, she had to do something about it. That is why she got up as best she could to beg the boss not to kill him out of mercy, that she would do whatever he wanted, anything, but that he would let him live. That unhappy man took advantage of her to quench his thirst for lust upon hearing her surrender before him, on her knees begging him to spare his life out of mercy.

The boss ordered them to throw him into the galley where Phillip had found them next to the river, without any food for three days, regardless of the condition he was in after the beating that the boss's cronies had given him.

Every time the boss did not like something, or he left the big house in a bad mood, he took it out on that poor couple by beating them until he thought they had killed them, then he ordered them to be locked up for three days to see if they would survive or not. Hatred burned his soul as he saw that each time he hit Seth, he miraculously recovered, despite the brutal conditions he faced with each beating.

The iniquitous man had developed the habit of abusing Ruth whenever he felt like it, no matter what condition she was in after the beating he gave her before raping her in front of Seth, whom he always tied to a post so he could see what he did with her.

Ruth told Elida that they had come to lose hope of being able to escape one day from that slavery of pain and suffering to which the lost and ignorant man chained them, but they had never lost faith.

Every night before the rapist stalked her, she began to pray on her knees imploring heaven for a little mercy, while Seth was tied to the post bleeding and unconscious because the boss sometimes sent his criminals to beat him up and tied him up, so he could abuse her after beating her almost unconscious.

Ruth told Elida that she felt some joy at having managed to escape after years of suffering, but that she felt sorry for those who had been left behind to continue to suffer the evil

136

with which some men pollute their hearts. Suddenly, Ruth wept because of the pain she felt, knowing what could happen to others because of them, when the boss realizes that they had escaped. She threw herself to the floor disconsolate because of the pain in her chest, screaming to God for a little mercy, asking the reason why he did not take pity on those poor people who suffered greatly in that miserable place, where justice did not protect the complaints of those abused by evil. She complained to God for his silence, for the lack of consolation when she called him asking for a little mercy, and she asked him if it was the case that he did not see them suffer, or if he did not care about their suffering.

Hearing the reproaches that Ruth misunderstood in her heart, Seth woke up believing that they was still in that place of anguish and suffering and tried to get out of bed by himself.

"Leave her alone," that poor man managed to say before falling to the floor, "leave her alone."

Elida prevented him from hitting his head on the edge of the iron bed, reacting quickly until she managed to take Seth's head with her hands, almost in a supernatural way. She then took him in her arms and put him back on the bed as if he were as light as a baby. Ruth was still lying on the floor being tortured by her reproaches, she could not do anything to help her. But the moment she realized what was happening, she immediately got up to hug Seth out of her joy that he was alive. She did not give much importance to the nature of what happened, because her mind was not willing to accept what she could not understand. She was overwhelmed only with the joy of seeing that her beloved had survived the merciless bitterness of all those years of suffering and pain.

Phillip went down for a minute because he had heard Ruth scream, but Elida calmed him down by saying not to worry, to go watch the ship's wheel, and that she would take care of the situation. She had to quickly explain to him just a few things that happened because Phillip did not look very convinced that she did not need his help, which seemed somewhat awkward to him. Looking deeply into her eyes for a few seconds, he recognized the security and courage with which Elida always faced things, and he trusted that his beloved was capable of taking care of herself, without any foreign intervention that could affect her perception of reality.

They passed through a town that was divided by the river, and just as he was returning to the cockpit, to take the wheel and turn off the lights quickly so no one could see them go under the bridge. "A ghost ship." Phillip managed to hear the voice of a child who was trying to alert others about the ship sailing down the Mississippi, but apparently no one listened to the unfortunate child.

After navigating for a few hours, they reached the river delta, where there was a town that sat just to the east, where some people could see them creeping by without any light. Phillip could see them from the cabin because they had a big bonfire lit on the riverbank, and he was sailing very close to where they were. Phillip decided that it was best to look for the furthest from the shore to avoid being seen. The stars were his only references, noticing the light of their glow on the dark night that covered that part of the planet.

Without any explanation other than the divinity guiding him through the unknown place, Phillip ventured as far as he could until he ran out of fuel to continue sailing. Not knowing what to do and finding no sign to guide him, he decided to strand himself on a small island to see if they could find somewhere safe to reconsider his next step.

Phillip got close enough to the island to avoid running aground, and he dropped the anchor so that the current would not carry them adrift down the river. He turned on the lights in the cabins to see that everyone was okay and alert them that they would stop because there was no more fuel to continue.

Walking towards the cabin where they had lodged the couple he had saved from that miserable place, he realized that Seth had improved, because he snored as if he had not slept in a long time, so he better decided to leave them alone so they could rest.

He found Elida with very tired eyes from not being able to sleep from waiting for him to come back to check on them. "Now that you're back, I'll rest a bit, bighead."

Phillip lay down on a cot that was on the floor next to the bed, after giving his beloved Emma a kiss on the forehead. He could not sleep because he was thinking about what to do to continue, so the first rays of the sun surprised him trying to find the reason why they had ended up stranded on an island in the middle of the river.

Uncertainty made him see how fragile they were without mercy from heaven, how miserable the hearts of men become far from grace, which fulfills its plans on time giving everyone an opportunity to learn a new experience as spirits. He thanked for the trust that had been placed in him, trusting that something would happen so that things would be easier for them and to be able to continue north, to be able to fulfill the mission for which they were destined since before they were born.

For some strange reason Phillip could not understand at that time, and because of that grace in which he blindly trusted, it began to snow heavily, covering the island in a matter of minutes.

Phillip was standing on the Amura de Br, amazed at the spectacle of seeing the snow fall for the first time.

After realizing it in his own way, he realized that he should hurry to remove some snow from the deck of the ship, as well as the cabins. So, he grabbed a shovel and set about trying to keep the boat as free of snow as possible. Although very soon he realized that it was foolish, since it was snowing so hard that it almost fell more than what he was taking away. He noticed Elida standing by the cabin window with Emma in her arms, showing her how apparently beautiful the snow looked.

Seeing Elida's smile and the joy of her daughter, he thought that this was the best moment of his life, seeing them laughing inside the cabin of the boat, seeing him try to remove the snow from the deck in vain.

He wished with all his heart that time did not pass so that he could enjoy their smiles as much as possible, but personal whims are not attended to base on the carnal ego, and the flow of time continued to delude him, until he understood that he should take care of finding the way to heat the ship's cabin, so they would not freeze at night.

He went to take a look at the cabin where Ruth and Seth were sleeping, to make sure they were okay, or if they needed anything. Upon entering, he looked at them curled up in bed, with a couple of blankets that Elida had given them to keep them warm, which she had found in the cabin where she and Emma slept. He noticed that Seth had eaten some of what Elida had given them, from the crumbs he had between his beards, so he felt calmer knowing that he would survive.

Seeing them sleeping in each other's arms as if they had not slept peacefully in a long time, he understood the difference between the apparent and the real. The most significant thing that he could have learned from all that experience, from its sublime details that divinity squanders among our vicissitudes, is that The Creator deals with his affairs in a way that man cannot understand, due to the limit that fear causes in his being, but he takes pity on the weakest and most vulnerable in a way that not even themselves understand.

Scouting the ship for something useful, he found three containers with enough fuel to travel much farther. He felt

140

that feeling that they should continue despite the weather conditions because the ship's owners would soon realize that it was no longer at the dock, and they would surely go looking for it. He arrived at the cabin where his loved ones were, so Moonlight rushed to hug him.

"Daddy, daddy, daddy!" Emma yelled as she saw him enter.

She gave him lots of kisses all over his face, then snuggled into his chest as he picked her up.

Phillip wanted to talk to Elida about leaving as soon as possible, but she interrupted him by telling him that he should eat something before doing anything, since she had already prepared something so they could eat together when he returned. Phillip took a moment to try some food, but only so that his beloved would not worry.

Elida supported him in all the decisions he made, without even hesitating that Phillip was right, trying by all means to protect them from tyrants and murderers, who were always thirsty to unleash their fury on the innocent.

The cold increased with the passing of the hours, due to that storm that had suddenly arisen over that region. Elida helped him load the fuel, then immediately started the boat so he could get out of the snow that was beginning to accumulate around.

The noise of the engines woke Ruth and Seth, who appeared in the cabin with their faces full of immense happiness, despite the wounds that were still open. Phillip helped Seth to sit in a chair so that he would not have to exert himself so much since he considered that he was still in very bad shape.

For the first time in a long time, the cold made Seth's left eye open, thus reducing the swelling that had lasted for years, thanks to the frequent beatings he was subjected to.

Seth did not care much about what was really happening, nor did he have any reproach in his heart that made him lose the opportunity to enjoy that feeling of freedom, which made him smile like a child. Phillip admired the strength of that man, who was firm and strong despite the injuries he had on his body.

After offering them something to eat and drink, Seth told them of the others who had been left behind on the galleys, enslaved by the tyrant. In addition that the ship in which they traveled was used to bring more slaves that could serve the boss.

He told them that it had been a true miracle that they were able to escape because Phillip and his family were destined for the same thing that they had suffered for so long.

They talked for several hours before taking Seth to lie down a bit so he could rest, since, although he appeared to be very strong, he was not quite well yet.

It took them two days to get to what seemed to be a big city, where according to Phillip they could have more job opportunities, and it would be more difficult for them to be tracked down to that mysterious city, which seemed enchanted by the sound of blues and jazz that it was heard on the banks of the river as they approached.

Phillip went to starboard immediately when he realized that the river got divided, and he felt that he should head towards that place that called to him with the wind and its jazz melody, which seduced him into a deep meditation on what that city was trying to warn him or teach him. Following his intuition, he let the mysterious magic of divinity guide them as far as they had to go.

There was a big old sign that said, Valero Memphis Refinery, where they stuck at the pier to abandon ship as soon as possible, fearing that the owner of the ship was looking for them to kill them. Or worse, take them to his galleys to abuse them for the rest of their undervalued lives.

Elida carried Emma and a bag that her grandmother had given her to keep little Moonlight's things, while Phillip carried the other three suitcases. Ruth helped Seth to walk, but he insisted that he could walk on his own, that he even asked Phillip if he wanted to help him with one of the suitcases. Phillip, respecting the intention with which Seth offered himself, gave him his backpack to help him carry it, since it was enough weight with the three suitcases, he gave it to him to take it. When Seth tried to carry it, he ended up on the ground along with the backpack next to Phillip, turning to see Phillip at that moment with a scared face that turned pale, because Phillip had given it to him with one hand as if it did not weigh that much. Phillip believed that he was still too weak to carry so much weight, for the truth is a burden that not everyone can carry so easily. Phillip took his backpack again and put it around his neck, so he can carry two of the suitcases, then he gave the lighter one to Seth so he would not feel useless, and he could continue healing sooner with his intention to be stronger every time. Ruth always accompanied him all the time to keep an eye on him, since he was still very hurt and feared that he might suffer a relapse.

Upon disembarking at the dock and without anyone noticing, they walked to the mainland where Phillip led them to the forest where the subliminal music came from, which seduced him by drawing him into its vibrant spell.

While walking a little through the forest, a beautiful woman with brown skin was sitting on a stone in a small moor where the evening light came in a little, making the woman's skin appear with a goldish skin color, while humming a song that she accompanied with the sound of her guitar.

They stopped when they entered the moor to not interrupt the beautiful melody, amazed at the golden glow that faded as the sun disappeared among the trees.

Little Moonlight almost jumped out of her mother's arms to run where that radiant woman was, who smiled to see them. The woman left her guitar next to her to carry little

Emma in her arms because Emma ran towards her with the same joy with which she ran into the arms of her father when she saw him arrive. It amazed everyone the way they hugged each other, while hundreds of butterflies flew around. The butterflies turned into dry leaves from the trees, which fell to the ground at the moment that they moved away circling with joy throughout that small subliminal moor.

Chapter 8
The Foreigners

Elida and Phillip approached them with the uncertainty of not knowing who the mysterious woman was, who seemed to know Emma very well. In the same way, little Moonlight showed the same enthusiasm that it feels when seeing a loved one again after a long time, at the moment when they hugged and laughed for the joy of seeing each other again. No one could deny this complicity, much less the love they reflected.

Both of them were confused because they did not remember having any visions about that moment, so they had no idea what was to come, so they had no choice but to wait and learn from whatever was to come.

Holding hands, they presented themselves before that beautiful woman, who did not stop smiling when she saw that they were approaching. "Lizzie D.," the mystery woman said.

She asked them for serenity and patience when uncertainty came to dominate them, and she told them that there was nothing to fear. On the contrary, they should be grateful for the benevolence of their protectors, who had already provided a safe place for them to stay. She reiterated to them that she would lead them to the indicated place where someone else would pick them up to take them to a place where they can rest.

She looked with great tenderness at Ruth, who was almost carrying Seth, because the poor innocent guy and badly injured still felt very weak, so she immediately went to help him carry him to the rock where she was playing the guitar. They laid him down a bit on the stone, at the moment when a

145

sudden breeze blew up the leaves, which turned into bright butterflies flying around Seth. Then, and to everyone's astonishment, after fulfilling their purpose, the butterflies returned to the ground to take their place in the dust, from which our bones and aching flesh are formed.

The last ray of the sun still hung from the top of the largest tree, from where a cloud of golden light descended, which positioned itself over Seth's body, then slowly descended until it healed all the wounds on his body.

Ruth was baffled by what she saw, falling to her knees at what was happening, clasping her hands on her chest as if asking for forgiveness for her transgressions and reproaches against the will of the divine.

"Forgive me, daddy," Ruth begged the sky.

"Our father is benevolent and pious," Lizzie D. asked her. "Get up and be worthy of his love."

The beautiful Lizzie turned to see Elida and asked her to give her the fruit that she kept in Emma's bag, which Mrs. Asia had given her on the silver tray, precisely so that she could use it in situations like this. Elida took out the fruit and passed it without hesitation to Lizzie, who took it with both hands.

When she squeezed it, a luminous juice came out, which she gave to Seth to drink. Seth got up a minute after having tasted that manna juice, as if nothing had happened to him, without any trace of the injuries he had on his body.

The golden light came out of his body, so Seth fell on his knees, thanking for the mercy with which he had been awarded, crying for the warmth that light caused in his heart, making him see the difference between good and evil.

As soon as the light was gone, it was dark, with Venus being the first to appear, then some constellations that stood out from the rest of the night sky. Then the super full moon came out illuminating the entire city. While admiring such a grand presentation of mystical dance, so that the night can reign in our dreams, they did not realize how or when Lizzie had disappeared. She had left with the prevailing light of the full moon, calling her in her new spiritual stage. Leaving everyone baffled without knowing what to do or where to go, since they did not know a single person who lived in that mystical city.

Little Moonlight was smiling, staring up at the moon, which was illuminating a path where a luminous breeze could be seen fluttering over the fallen leaves.

Without any fear in their hearts, they headed down the path following the breeze that guided them to the edge of the forest, where a couple of people were looking for a suitable place where they could meditate a bit.

These two natives of the land were looking for answers to all the concerns that tormented their hearts, in a place away from the bustle of the city, hoping to find the answer that could give them some type of hope that not all was lost.

These two intrepid noble youths were surprised to see them leaving the path of the forest, trying not to be seen. That made them think that maybe they were criminals trying to get away from their misdeeds.

As they got close enough to see Elida carrying little Emma, they realized they were foreigners; even so, they did not discriminate against them by misjudging them.

On the contrary, those noble youths offered to help them carry their suitcases, in addition to telling them about a place where they could stay for the night, because everything was about to freeze, and it was very dangerous to be exposed to these conditions for a long time.

One of the young men told Phillip that if they stayed out in the open for a couple more hours they would surely freeze to death. You do not need to be too smart to know that those young men were right.

They told them not to be afraid because the place they were referring to belonged to a very good lady, who always gave lodging to everyone who came to her house, who would surely receive them without problems.

Ruth was somewhat nervous at the thought that they might want to assault them, or worse, that they wanted to enslave them or abuse them. Seth calmed her down a bit, telling her not to be afraid of them, that she should trust Phillip's good judgment to decide what to do.

Elida turned to see Phillip instantly to look for a sign that would give her the confidence she needed at that moment; Well, she knew that those natives were right, warning them that they could freeze to death if they stayed longer in the forest. Phillip trusted in his heart that those young people were telling the truth, so he asked everyone not to worry, that they would be fine in the shelter.

That old widow named Vicky Rey received them at her house so that they could stay as long as necessary, and she asked Elida to allow her to carry Emma to take her to a room in the house where it was warmer, because the cold was almost unbearable at that moment.

Elida and Vicky Rey stayed in the room for a while, while they put Emma on a bed to sleep. The others waited in the living room complaining about how good the warmth of the fireplace felt. As they left the room where little Moonlight was sleeping, Vicky Rey said, "Prends bien soin d'elle, Margarita." Elida had not seen anyone else in the room when they entered, but she did catch a glimpse of a little girl, about six years old, who was sitting on the bed next to Emma, just as Vicky Rey closed the door.

One of the young natives was the one who translated everything that Mrs. Vicky Rey told them, as well as introducing them to all the other tenants, who were happy to meet them. Elida was the only one who understood everything they said, because she had had classes in that language. They gave them a room and something to eat to ease their sorrows a bit. They helped them arrange their things and gave them some clothes, especially some coats and socks because the cold was unbearable at that time.

Phillip knew that the cold would intensify as they traveled further north, so he considered staying for a while until weather conditions allowed them to resume their journey.

As the days went by, the pressure of finding a job to provide something for his loved ones assaulted Phillip. He had the idea of teaching some of those who lived in the house to fix things so that they could fend for themselves, and thus they would help him to form a work group. In the same way, Elida taught the women to cook different dishes of food, to offer them in the office buildings, and thus be able to get money to cover the expenses of Vicky Rey's house.

Very soon they earned the respect of all, for the great work and effort they showed helping the community that had welcomed them.

Phillip, helped by Seth and some of those who lived in the house, set up a mechanical workshop in one of the sheds in the backyard, which quickly became very popular due to the efficiency and honesty with which they always treated each job.

Elida's food had become famous in all the buildings in the center of the city, for the unique flavor that she gave to the dishes she prepared. She knew endless recipes from all over the world that her mother had taught her, which were inherited from her grandmother. With the help of Ruth, who became her best friend, they worked very early in the morning cooking the orders that the offices made and then delivered them at lunchtime by the other women who lived in Mrs. Vicky Rey's house.

The young and always smiling Vinicius Clay, was the one who drove the truck they used to distribute food between the office buildings, as well as protecting them from those who are always looking to take what does not belong to them. Many are victims of adverse circumstances resulting from bad government, not having the means or education enough to fend for themselves. It does not mean that this is the excuse that supports their abuse, their lack of respect for the rights of others, or the property of others. We know that there are no social programs that help young people, or anyone to rediscover their true potential, because governments do not care about things like that, they care about the economic and political systems.

They protect big companies and banks, but the poor are only required to pay taxes. Are precisely these last ones who maintain these economic systems but lack the resources and means to grow as individuals.

The community felt comfortable with Phillip's advice, so on many occasions on Sundays at the local church service they asked him to come to the pulpit to speak.

They were never discriminated against because of their skin color, or the size of their body, or the complex language they spoke.

Emma had won the affection of everyone on the block where they lived, for the sympathy and good heart she had with all the children in the neighborhood, whom she always hugged and kissed on the cheek when their parents took them to visit them to Mrs. Vicky Rey's house.

Those months were a great blessing for everyone in the neighborhood, especially for Seth and Ruth, who found in that place the opportunity they wanted for a long time, and which they did not waste in the slightest when they decided to stay and live forever in that neighborhood, to finally be able to start a new life.

They still had faith that one day they could be reunited with their children, after so many years of suffering and torture. It was the kindness and good heart of many in the community that encouraged them to resume that dream lost due to injustice and discrimination. Now the divinity played its part to reward pain and sorrow, by placing them in the midst of noble and kind beings who appreciated their way of being, without judging their appearance or hurting their sympathy and honesty.

They had to change their names like Elida and Phillip, so that no one would ever find a relationship with their past, and thus the corrupt misers would seek them out to make them disappear.

Although very soon they realized that the name had no relevance, when appreciating what each person has within their spirit; Well, the values learned from home are made known in the actions with which the spirit of each person is conducted when trying to help others, or simply by being themselves.

Thanks to the construction techniques that Phillip had taught three of the tenants of Mrs. Vicky Rey's house, and two more who lived on the same street, they were able to expand the house in the following months to accommodate more people who needed food or shelter. The boys supported him when Phillip asked if they wanted to form a small construction business. He told them that they could start offering their work to small projects for a fair and reasonable price, to show that they were capable of doing it well, nicely, and cheaply. Some were not quite sure how nice Phillip's plan sounded, because they thought no one would hire them because they were black. Phillip encouraged them to trust themselves, telling them that appearances are deceptive, that the fear of being rejected was just one more barrier, which prevented their spirits from shining among the most respectable citizens of this great nation.

With the example of his actions and the undeniable power of his words, Phillip demonstrated the simple and noble heart that he possessed, by always being willing to help others without judging people's idea or way of living.

On Thursday afternoons they would go out looking for things among the garbage of middle-class neighborhoods, to take them to the neighborhood where they lived and give it to low-income people. Whenever he found toys among the garbage, Phillip said that this was the only reason he liked to do community service, because he imagined the children's smiles upon receiving that toy. The ones that were broken were repaired by Phillip with great joy, thinking that he would cause great enthusiasm by giving it to Emma, or some other kid on the block, so that they could enjoy their childhood fantasizing about a sweet and eternal reality.

Elida met with all the girls on the block to talk to them about mutual respect between people, charity, and the good manners of helping with any form of service.

Many of them were young girls who had been raped and mistreated by racist people, who sometimes came out of their trenches to claim the lie with which their poor and ignorant idolatry is suggested; Well, the supposed superiority that their clan claims do not show signs of a spiritually higher level, in accordance with the primitive actions with which they try to demonstrate their ignorance and their fears.

Elida told them on many occasions that those deceived were the true slaves in the world, not having enough education and spiritual strength to realize the lie in which they waste their lives on.

Poor naive people, they have not given themselves the opportunity to grow in self-awareness, so that one day they could meet again and realize the earthly error to which they are being dragged, by petty interests of those who try to dominate the population of this world.

Ruth and other young women from the block supported her with the idea of forming a league that would seek justice and dignity among the communities in that part of the city, which lacked public services, as well as rights and opportunities to earn a dignified life like any other citizen.

Elida encouraged them to face injustice with a less submissive character, to defend the rights of human dignity,

152

and seek a future where equality between people is respected. Not only in this great northern nation, but throughout the world. She always insisted on the great potential that she appreciated in them, so that they would not remain just like a frustrated dream, but rather so that each one defended the right to be and to think in freedom and respect for truth and love.

They had meetings every weekend before their service at the community church, where they helped prepare food for the homeless who lined up outside the church to receive a piece of bread and some rice pudding.

They took advantage of the occasion to distribute flyers to the homeless, to promote the idea among the community, and thus make people aware of the rights to which they were creditors.

Elida had no idea of the history behind this primitive instinct that incited some to commit acts of stupidity and ignorance and believed that their fight should not be difficult if what they demanded was justice and truth. Two things that obviously have not prevailed in this new order of domination and control over the population of this planet. Each one judge in your own way.

Vicky Rey's house was an unofficial daycare, which helped take care of the children of people who had to work, or who did not have enough resources to hire a babysitter to take care of the children while they went out to search for daily bread. Vicky Rey taught the younger children to read, as well as entertaining them with stories that she had learned from her grandmother, and many other activities that she enjoyed sharing with those little children.

Many of the parents sent their children to Vicky Rey's house, just so they could eat something, because they did not even have enough for themselves.

These were difficult times for some of those who lived on that street, without work or help from any government institution that attended to the needs of its citizens. On the contrary, there was systematic and undeniable discrimination that segregated the poorest to live in misery and a lack of basic services. One would expect this among the poorest countries on the planet, but the truth is that it is a reality in supposedly first-world countries.

Today there are cities in these developed countries, in which thousands of homeless people roam, and without hope that their leaders will give them adequate attention to resolve the social discrepancy in which their misfortunes and their rights have no remedy.

Everyone points fingers at each other to blame for what is happening, but no one tries to solve the root of the problem. On the contrary, they try to cover the sun with one finger, by not properly addressing the problem by ignoring the true causes, because that way they would confront big companies, economic and political systems.

Nobody is willing to lose money, and nobody is willing to lose power.

There were no resources earmarked for these communities, nor respect from the rest of the population, because the primitive idea with which some boasted was simply that, a primitive instinct that called their uncivilization.

These ignorant and unjust lived deceived by the interests engineered by pride and hatred with which their leaders nourished and encouraged them, giving them no freedom or opportunity to be themselves.

Just like today, they were slaves to lies and falsehood, which always hurts the innocent who end up suffering discrimination and racism that refuse to disappear.

Drugs and alcohol consumed the young promises, who had no choice but to sell drugs or become an alcoholic or addicted to one of those poisons that consumes everyone who falls into their trap. The lack of opportunities that that community suffered, due to the fact of having a different skin color, prevented from taken advantage of the talent that many of these great young people had. Many good-quality intellectuals and artists were ignored for the simple fact of being black.

There is a lot of ignorance that exists when trying to judge others by the color of their skin, by the size of their body or the idea of their heart.

Especially if he ignores himself and how imperfect his vanity is and ignores the lie that the ego creates in his reason, in his idea of life.

All those months of celebrations and successes in all his projects surprised Phillip with the arrival of summer, making him a bit uncomfortable with the idea that he should continue his journey north, despite feeling at home, for all that sympathy and sincere friendship that he received from everyone in the community.

But, despite the fact that apparently everything was for the best, he felt a responsibility to continue his mission to move forward to face this mysterious cause. For the same strange reason that it had brought him to that place, where his personality stood out above racial and social prejudices, which hurt the union of this great nation of the north.

The mechanical workshop prospered greatly, to the point of having to demolish the warehouse that was in the backyard of Vicky Rey's house, to later build a workshop with better equipment and machinery to facilitate work and thus be able to guarantee safety from the workers.

Vicky Rey represented Phillip in all the official requirements by the city, to be able to open the workshop officially, since months after the word of their good job they were doing spread, an inspector went to ask them for the necessary permission to work in the business. Vicky Rey showed him all the documents and permits from the municipality, to be able to work the workshop and the food business; In addition, the construction team that Phillip had

155

formed with the young people of the house and some who lived on the same street, which began building the workshop and remodeling Vicky Rey's house, with more rooms so that more homeless people could have a dignified refuge in which to soothe their sorrows.

Elida and Phillip's nightly talks focused on the next step for the community to have more educational resources from the city.

They asked Vicky Rey and Vinicius Clay to represent them before the municipal president, because they planned to carry out a musical activity that would promote the good talent that existed in the community. Neither Vicky Rey nor Vinicius Clay could deny the pride they felt when they recognized the intention of Elida and Phillip, for which they accepted wholeheartedly, despite knowing the challenge that all of this meant.

They held a community meeting to discuss the proposal, with some stating that it would be virtually impossible for them to be allowed to do such a thing.

Elida and all the women of the Justice League helped to convince those unsecure that it would be a very important step to demonstrate the quality and talent of many of the youth in the community.

Those insecure few declared that they were not the ones against it, on the contrary, they were proud of the opportunity to demonstrate their qualities, but that they doubted the local authorities.

In the end, the entire community was enthusiastically committed to doing everything possible to make it happen.

Despite the thousand excuses that the municipality responded for not carrying out what they proposed, they managed to convince many of the delegates and representatives to join the project, almost to the point of protesting to be considered. For some very strange reason they managed to convince the authorities to approve the event, at the moment when they were about to lose hope. Phillip was convinced that this had been the work of the divine, because it was not possible to reason with those men, much less convince them that it was something good for the community.

They organized a huge music event that drew many more neighborhoods to participate, where Elida and the women from the Justice League handed out flyers inviting people to join the fight against social inequality, gender discrimination and racial hatred.

They organized a great campaign to obtain more resources and the necessary means to carry out all the good intentions they had for the community that had welcomed them with such affection, which assimilated them as part of themselves, upon discovering the sympathy their hearts had, as they dedicated their lives to serving and helping others.

Neither Phillip's talent nor Elida's good education went unnoticed in that neighborhood, much less Emma's charisma, and sympathy, who grew every day more among that community of noble and humble beings. Everyone adored her for the way she reflected the magic of her parents' good upbringing and the kindness of their heart.

Many intellectuals and talented people approached Phillip's advice, recognizing the great gift with which he had been awarded from the highest heaven.

The festival was a complete success, bringing many neighborhoods together to share and contribute to the cause that would benefit the community's musical talent.

Elida played a couple of jazz tunes with a group of musicians, with a pianola that a neighbor had lent her. Emma, seeing the drums that were on the stage, began to run to try to get some sound by hitting them with her hand. They were a pair of drums that a musician from the southern lands had brought to play a tune for the event, and which he had placed on the stage floor. The sympathy and innocence of little

Moonlight caused the applause of the people who gathered to listen to good music, seeing her trying to get a rhythm in tune with the broken words she was trying to say.

A representative of the municipality attended to verify that everything was under the rules, which had been stipulated in the permit that had been issued to carry out the event. The same one who informed his superiors of some irregularities that he had discovered in that event, regarding the businesses that Vicky Rey supposedly had. He realized something suspicious when he heard the thanks to Elida and Phillip, for their great dedication to helping the community, for them to come together to share good values, but, above all, to claim the rights that every person should have equally.

The inspector investigated the names of Elida and Phillip to make sure that his suspicions were true, since he believed that they were illegal immigrants.

He reported what he had discovered to his superior, and this did as well report them to the immigration department so that they could take action on the matter.

Days after the news of the big musical event began to spread throughout the state, four federal officers arrived at Vicky Rey's house looking for Phillip and Elida. Vinicius was the one who opened the door for them and replied that he did not know anyone with those names, that perhaps they had the wrong address.

The officers forced their way in because they already knew in advance from the municipal inspector that these people lived in that place. They searched every corner of the house for some clue, but they did not even find Phillip's suitcases and his beloved family. Since Phillip had had a vision the day before alerting him to what would happen, he asked Vicky Rey for her help so they can flee as soon as possible without anyone noticing.

They had one day to say goodbye to the good friends they had formed in that community, who sadly said goodbye to

158

them knowing that they would have to leave. Everyone knew that they were illegal immigrants; Even so, they were never judged or discriminated against in any way; on the contrary, they treated them as one of their own from the community.

They understood the situation they were going through and offered them their unconditional support. Vicky Rey warned some members of the community so that in the event that they were asked, they would deny knowing those people; and thus, protect the freedom of those who had made an honest effort and without interests, alien to the goodness of the spirit, to procure the right to equality and respect.

Phillip entrusted the mechanical workshop to Seth and Vinicius, trusting that they would take care of making it prosper even more than they had achieved up to then.

They promised him to continue with the same sense of integrity and dedication with which he had managed to convince them of what they did not know they were capable of doing, which they learned by seeing the example with which Phillip took great care in his daily tasks, helping those who had less.

Vicky Rey cried that afternoon when Elida said goodbye to her, and to all the great friends she had known and that now she would have to leave behind once again, to continue in the destiny marked out by the divine, on the path that the spirit has chosen to learn the experience of carnal life.

The sadness of losing a loved one was compared to the pain that Vicky Rey felt knowing that Elida would move away from her, and that perhaps she would never see her again; for, she had come to love her and Emma as her daughter and granddaughter that she had lost.

In those times and places, social injustice reigned everywhere, allowing racial prejudice to spread without anyone being able to do anything.

Vicky Rey lost her family on one of those nights when some peasants from the area who were drunk looking for fun in the city, kidnapped her daughter and granddaughter while they were walking along the riverbank.

They raped them and then cruelly mercilessly murdered them. They dumped their bodies near the forest where Vinicius Clay had found Phillip's family and the Chipilín, on that cold winter night, when they got off the boat to seek refuge. It was a pity that Vicky Rey's daughter and granddaughter did not have the same luck.

The authorities never tried to arrest the culprits, despite knowing the whereabouts of all those wretches, just because they were white. They were not even given a trial, and none of them went to jail for a single day, because the judge declared them mentally ill who did not know what they were doing.

Vicky Rey, despite having sworn never in her life to cry again, because she had already cried enough tears to realize that justice would never be done regarding her private pain, for having lost the beings she loved the most in life, she cried very sadly when she knew that they would move away from her. She knew that not even divine justice could bring her family back, and that in this world there was no room for equality or justice.

Elida was the one who made her believe again in hope and in eternal love, which does not die with the flesh of those we love. That is why she cried inconsolably as she accepted the departure of those she had come to love as her own family.

Ruth and the other young women who lived in the house joined in a big hug around them, because of the great affection they had for her, not only for teaching them endless different dishes of food from all parts of the world, but also for the grace with which her spirit boasted of loving them in a very good way, treating them as if they were her own sisters.

Ruth fell on her knees in front of Phillip to thank him for having saved them that night when they were captives in that miserable place. Phillip put his hand on her forehead, so Ruth

160

stopped crying, then closed her eyes, and a happy smile could be seen that embellished her face, at the moment when a warm wind wrapped around her, wiping her tears. "I'm sorry, daddy." Ruth exclaimed.

All that time that Phillip lived with them, Seth had got to know him a little better than the others, and he had a very different affection of gratitude from the one that the others had for him; Well, he had saved their lives, taught humility, and honest work. Above all, the good habit of helping those most in need, whether material or spiritual.

Seth hugged him crying with great joy for having met him and told him that he would never stop thanking him for how generous he had been with them, so he would have his unconditional friendship for whatever he might need.

Seth knelt before Phillip, at the precise moment when he was calling him master, but Phillip stopped him with one hand and asked him to prostrate himself with dignity because there was no reason to prostrate himself before him; Well, there was no difference between what one or the other was capable of doing. He told him that his path would be one of many trials, but to be diligent with service and humility so that he would not fall into the whims of ego or vanity.

The other tenants were not very surprised to see the affection that some had for them, because they had realized the reward with which the creator had blessed them, with his friendly and cheerful way of being, and the excessive impudence for always wanting to help the neediest.

The food business and the workshop made very good profits, which they used to help the homeless in the city with food, and especially the neediest in the neighborhood, offering financial help to pay for medical expenses and medicine.

Elida ran both businesses, despite cooking and tending to Justice League business. She taught Ruth how to take care of business finances, a month before they decided to head north once more; Well, Elida had had a dream that warned her of certain things that were not entirely clear in her mind, but that she later related in her nightly talks to the moment they should leave. In the same way Phillip did with the mechanical workshop, confidently leaving it with his two great friends. Vicky Rey promised them that she would take care of them as if they were her own children.

The pain of parting was a big deal, to the point of begging them not to do it, because they would protect them from anything. Elida and Phillip did not deny that it was possible, but neither did they deny that they could receive reprisals because of them, and that was precisely what they wanted to avoid. In the end, they all respected the decision they had already made; by giving them the last thing they could give them, the blessing, and the wish that they do well in everything they set out to do in life. But if they wanted to return one day, they would not doubt that they had their home in that place.

A cousin of Vinicius was the one who took them to Lebanon, where they would meet an acquaintance of Vicky Rey to ask him to allow them to stay at his house. Vinicius's cousin, named Cassius Clay, offered them something to eat when they arrived in town, in a small restaurant on the main avenue.

They waited there for more than two hours for the person who would pick them up, but no one came.

Young Cassius reminded them that he was on his way back to his house, that if they wanted, they would be welcomed in Kentucky, because his old house had enough space for them to stay as long as they wanted. Phillip thanked him very cordially for the intention, but they would stay to wait for the person that Vicky Rey had recommended to them. That, in the event of needing his help, they would look for him at the right time, but that if he wanted to continue to get back to his old house in Kentucky, he would do it without any worries. He thanked her once more for the offer, then Cassius said goodbye to them and left.

They waited until the owner of the restaurant asked them if they had just arrived, seeing the suitcases next to the table where they still had some food, because Emma always took her time to eat things, that sometimes even the food got cold before finishing her plate.

The owner of the restaurant immediately asked one of the waitresses to pick up the plates and warm up what the little girl had on the plate. The waitress collected the dishes and cleared the table, then the owner called her over and whispered something in her ear. A few minutes later, the waitress returned with three nicely served dishes to go.

The owner told them that they were about to close the place that if they had an address or phone number of the person they were waiting for. Phillip and Elida thanked him for the gesture and replied no, only that they would see him in front of the restaurant that day six hours ago.

The owner of the restaurant named José Pérez López, told them that he had a small room in the back of the restaurant that could serve as a refuge for that night, that if they wanted, they could stay, and in the morning, they would decide what to do. Phillip accepted and thanked him wholeheartedly for the great gesture of goodwill that he had towards them, who were strangers to him, but who helped them as any other countryman would do for anyone.

While Elida and little Emma settled in the little room to rest a bit, Phillip stayed with José helping him clear the tables and wash the dishes so he could pay him a little for letting them stay on his property. They talked long enough for José to realize Phillip's kindness and good heart, feeling in his chest a sensation of comfort at being by his side listening to what Phillip felt he could entrust to him.

There were more and more words from little Emma, who grew up in the midst of her parents' nomadic life, always having to flee from the poisonous claws of the beast that feeds the ambition for power and control of the truth. She sometimes told her mother not to worry about her, with those innocent childish words, because she would always be by her side; In addition, she reminded Phillip that she loved him, just when he sheltered her and gave her a good night kiss.

"I love you too my bud of love," Phillip answered with a sincere heart.

A voice in one of his dreams woke up Phillip at half past three in the morning, which insistently called his name. Even when he realized that he was awake he kept hearing the voice, but this time he recognized that it was The Old Lady with the White Hair. He got out of bed and walked to the window to watch the moon, thinking that maybe it was the same voice that he sometimes heard.

The moonlight carried the old lady's message about those left behind in their homeland, where they had to flee to protect the truth from corrupted puppets who betrayed their own kind. This may not be very clear to many, but in this world, there are men in collusion with the dark to carry out atrocities even against their own brothers. It is greed over greed that still blinds the conscience of many of them, that is why there is still no freedom or enlightenment in this world.

Raúl had learned to channel himself through the old lady, to be able to give information to Phillip about what had happened with the grandmother, and the problems they had in the mansion.

The grandmother had fallen ill because they had tried to poison her in a restaurant in the city of the state. It was feared that it had been Elida's stepfather so that he could keep the inheritance that corresponded to her mother. The grandmother recovered because she was of very good blood, and for the care that everyone gave her in those days when they thought they would lose her. When Phillip got lost a bit in the shadows, he thought about the medallion and the gold pectoral, believing that with them he would be invincible before the ignorant fools who do not know the good the spirit could teach them. The energy in his belly told him that anger led to hate, and that grudge would be his next step to understand before continuing on his path.

"No one is guilty, only me." Philip thought.

Understanding how imperfect he was at the moment of judging others for their own pain, he wondered how it was possible that he had not realized how wrong he was, wanting to eliminate those who did not quite understand the miraculous and wonderful fact of just being alive.

He felt incomplete and ignorant of how much he still had to learn about life and the vicissitudes of the spirit, so he accepted that he was not yet ready to teach his brothers to continue on the right path of truth.

Looking at the moon and the shadows it created on things, he understood that he did not have enough wisdom to ensure what was fair for some and what was not correct for others. So, he simply resigned himself to wait for the moments that could teach him what he needed to know, to find the answer to why God had decided to eliminate most of his creation, to correct the mistakes he had made with his own intentions.

He had that idea insistently in his thoughts, that with The Tools of Order he could eliminate the ignorant iniquitous who caused pain in the world; Well, if God had done it as its creator, then it was a viable action to start over as a more self-aware civilization. Suddenly he heard Gabriel's voice inside him, resounding to him as if the interior of him were a great empty room, which told him, "All at its own time, Phillip."

_jema_sid

Chapter 9
The Beginning Of Calvary

Phillip cried when he recognized Gabriel's voice, and when he remembered his promise that he would never leave him alone in any moment of need. At that moment Elida woke up and called him back to bed, so he could try to get some rest before dawn, because they should be as strong as ever to face whatever the day might bring before them.

He felt proud to have her support and understanding, so he took what her beloved told him very seriously. He was still somewhat worried about what had happened with Elida's grandmother, and he was not too sure about telling her.

He stayed for a moment thinking very well about the best thing he could do to protect them from any harm, but he could not find any guarantee that everything would be fine, so he resigned himself to the divines' will.

Phillip went back to bed next to his loved ones, especially not to worry Elida more than she already was because of everything they had been through.

Before falling asleep, he remembered something Raúl had told him about Marcelino, Elida's uncle, who knew a good friend in those lands. That in the event that they could get there, they could trust that he would help them in any way possible.

It was a surprisingly obvious coincidence, the fact that they were precisely in those lands where Marcelino's friend lived. Nothing seemed strange to him anymore at this stage of the road, where he was sure that the divine acted in favor of goodness and justice. He knew that nothing was limited to luck or coincidence, so he just had to wait for the way things would unfold.

A couple of hours later, Elida and Emma woke up as they usually do during that time, trying not to make noise so Phillip could sleep a few more minutes, while Elida fixed some things, and took some clean clothes out of one of the suitcases, from which fell one of the luminous fruits, which Emma took and began to eat. After eating half of the fruit, she gave her mother the other half, which Elida cut in two, ate one slice of it, and left the other for Phillip when he wakes up.

The noise that the door of the restaurant caused when it opened it woke up Phillip, but he did not get up right away, he remained calm and carefree for a minute. That worried Elida a bit since this was not the time to relax. Phillip sat on the edge of the bed for a few seconds, then stood up to give each of them a hug and a kiss, who smiled at him when their eyes crossed each other after waking up.

The restaurant owner told them that he could not give them both work, because he already had all the positions filled, except washing the dishes. He told Phillip if he wanted Elida to stay in that position, and that he would find him a job with some boys from town who go to work in tobacco or construction. Elida accepted in a good way, happy to be able to help a little.

Phillip went to work with the boys, friends of José, at the ranch where they were building some sheds to hang the tobacco after cutting it.

The ranch owner, a cheerful and simple man named Wayne Taylor, turned out to be the person Raúl was referring to in his message. Phillip realized when he heard the name of Mr. Taylor by one of the workers, who was traveling together with him in the back of the small truck, to go to work in the area between Chattanooga and Lebanon, where Mr. Wayne Taylor's ranch was. The boys introduced him to Mr. Taylor,

Phillip asked if he could talk to him for a minute, because he had something important to tell him about his good friend Marcelino.

Mr. Taylor remembered his old friend very fondly and recalled those days at the university when they were young, researching all kinds of jobs together. He was very pleased to have heard that his good friend had become what he always tried to be, a good man dedicated to protecting and ensuring justice among people. He promised to give him work for as long as he deemed prudent, and that he counted on his help just as the others had always counted on him, without any distinction of gender or race, religious or political ideology.

Phillip thanked him for his trust and promised to do his best to show that he was capable of working in the fields like any other. That he would not regret it.

The advantage they had that Elida worked in the restaurant was that the owner had allowed her to have her daughter around to take care of her, since it did not require much work to wash the dishes, and thus she would have the time to take care of her as much as possible, furthermore, they did not know anyone whom they could entrust the care of little Moonlight.

Phillip thought that this was an advantage for her, since being independent and self-sufficient was always the best thing she knew how to do in her life, apart from loving and protecting the most in need. Although Phillip felt that she could protect and care for Emma better than anyone else, because if she did not work, she could educate her better, giving her more time to teach her the good values that are always learned at home.

This should not be confused with the irrational masculinity with which many men try to enslave female abilities, because Phillip knew that Elida was much more capable than that, but he believed that if she gave Moonlight more time, then the little girl could enjoy a little more the warmth and teaching of her mother. Knowing how much he had missed his mother, that is why he tried to ensure that his daughter did not suffer the same way he had. He always respected Elida's decisions and never limited her skill or creative capacity. On the contrary, he always admired her sense of courage with which she faced any problem. And as soon as he had the opportunity, he told her that she was much stronger than him, because she was really the one who supported the three of them in the midst of all that unfair chaos that life presented them on the road. He never denied her the admiration he felt for her; especially how much he loved her.

Over time, monotony caught both of them at the crossroads of jealousy, the envy of others, and the unjustified resentment of ignorance. As our own lesson so that we learn how weak we are in the face of the incomprehensible of life, in the face of adversity that refuses to abandon its part. Each one judge in your own way.

In the restaurant, the excessive and very apparent attention on the part of the owner towards Elida unleashed the envy of others, causing them to invent rumors and gossip about what was mysteriously happening between José and Elida. She did not tell Phillip what was happening so that he would not worry, not fearing that Phillip would get angry or doubt her fidelity, but so that he would not waste time on other people's weaknesses and doubts.

Elida's love was real and unbreakable, there was no way she would let herself be carried away by doubts, or by the gossip that others did out of envy of her sweet and honest personality. In the same way, Phillip did not have his capacity limited by ignorance, nor was his heart contaminated with the irrational jealousy with which many of us fall due to fear and insecurity.

He was aware of everything that was happening, but nevertheless he never wanted to say anything about it, since he faithfully believed that it was not worth wasting the few opportunities they had to live in peace.

The love they felt for each other was much stronger than any gossip or other people's envy. It was precisely for this reason that Phillip always tried to protect his loved ones from the insecurities with which men tend to waste their lives on.

In one way or another they managed to ignore the insistent petty insinuations on the part of those whom envy killed. That caused the uncontrollable hatred of those ignorant people, seeing that they were not affected by the slander with which they used to try to harm them. Without a doubt, they had to swallow their pride in the face of the love and incorruptible trust that Phillip and Elida exuded, by simply living without prejudice or doubt.

Months passed until they celebrated Emma's second birthday, at a small birthday party they organized in the restaurant, along with very few new friends who decided to accompany them.

Good friends are always present at the right moments to provide the support that is needed, without judging the gossip that the envious invent to quench their grudges.

Over time, Phillip realized that his honest and fair work was envied by some who always tried to make him look bad with Mr. Wayne.

Phillip always finished cutting the tobacco sooner than anyone else, the same was true during planting season. This meant that many did not like that he earned more than them, despite the fact that they had more time than him cutting tobacco. For this reason, and because of the lowliness that envy causes, when Phillip went to eat, they looted his bales to say it was theirs.

Anything was enough for those envious to attack him and try in some way to make him look bad with the boss. And boy did they try in a thousand ways to conspire against him, but even so they could not do anything to make the boss believe everything they invented.

Mr. Wayne was not stupid, he knew perfectly well the capacity of Phillip, who despite suffering the slanders of others, never betrayed him. Nor did Mr. Wayne say anything to the unjustified complaints of other workers, because the good honest work with which Phillip always stood out, endorsed him as the responsible and honest man that he was. The envious had no choice but to swallow their pride and courage by not achieving their bad intentions, although they never stopped insisting to try to harm him.

The gossip that had been invented about his beloved, Phillip discovered that they had been slandered by two of his co-workers. The same insecure and ignorant ones who always tried to say things about him. He just ignored them.

Having nothing to hide or fear, Elida told Phillip about the insecurities that blinded the envious, for which he told her that he was aware of everything that was happening, that she had nothing to worry about. In any case, it was necessary to talk about it so that there was no doubt on both ends. Their nocturnal talks centered on the best ways they could do to avoid the absurd attacks of the ignorant bastards.

Emma learned to speak with the same cadence and accent as her mother, and she was already aware of the rumors that people maliciously formed about Elida's innocence and Phillip's kindness. For this reason and many other things that happened to them, Phillip and Elida decided to leave and go to a town called Hendersonville with some friends they had met at a yard sale. And to those who tried whenever they could to spend a weekend or holiday with them.

There is no doubt that good people always act according to their hearts, just like good friends do to help us with whatever is offered to us.

Everyone who has a sincere friendship knows that it is an invaluable and unshakable treasure in the face of adversity.

And you will not let me lie when I say that on many occasions true friends become even more than our own brothers.

They stayed in a small room on the roof of the apartment building where their friends lived, which had a bathroom and a small kitchen. Phillip and Elida found that place more than enough, which, although it was very humble, was a privilege that many lack. Besides, it was similar enough to the opportunity where they could get closer to their dream of being able to form a permanent home.

Julio Chávez was the name of his great friend who was married to a young blonde daughter of a rancher in the region. They had two children almost the same age as Emma, only differing by a few months.

Joy Wittman, who worked with the county sheriff, had married Julio so that he could fix his immigration status, but the truth was that they had fallen in love from the first moment they met, and they did not hesitate to start a family, regardless of the complexes with which people are deceived to discriminate against the poorest or the neediest. It was not easy to convince Joy's parents to allow her to marry Julio, since foreigners were not very well seen or accepted in that region. Much less that he married a young woman from the region. Many opposed the wedding taking place, almost to the point of protesting that they could not do it in any of the churches in the region.

The same thing happened in the civil registry, where the requirements became almost impossible for José. Joy had to have a serious conversation with her parents first, then she held a community meeting to tell them that whatever they did, they would not prevent the love they felt for each other. Some objected despite what Joy told them, but they had no choice but to accept that this is what was going to happen.

Over time, the community realized the good heart that Julio had, so little by little they accepted him as one of them.

Above all, because good values and principles are things that cannot be hidden.

Phillip continued to work in construction with some boys who lived in that town, between the Central City area and Elizabethtown.

He practically worked at anything, from cleaning the patios of rich houses to feeding the cattle on a ranch in the region. This time, he preferred to keep a low profile, which would not attract the attention of those who like to maintain the power to manipulate the feelings of the population; Well, he could not allow himself to put his loved ones at risk again.

Phillip lived a peaceful life since then, where he limited himself only on obeying the orders that the contractors gave him in the works, in which he enjoyed learning new things.

After a few years in Hendersonville, he found what he was always looking for, freedom and the opportunity to forget what his destiny had indelibly marked on his path. He tried to ignore what his being told him insistently every day when he left for work.

Seeing his loved ones happy and carefree of what they had experienced, it made him think that if he ignored the spiritual, he could live like anyone else without prejudices or mystical objectives on his shoulders, that spoil all those moments that we waste on banal ideas every day.

He came to want a simple life and far from anything the divine wanted. At the very least, he refused to accept that his family was marked to fulfill the whims of a creator that he had erred and now tried to make up for his fault with the lives of the innocent.

Despite what he had already discovered about the truth of life and the spirit, he imagined living his last days next to his family without caring what might happen to others.

Elida took care of Emma when she came home from school and used the time to knit baby clothes in the mornings when Phillip went to work. They had agreed that she would

174

not work this time, but it was almost impossible for the way she was. So, she quickly adapted to the circumstances, selling the little jackets that her grandmother had taught her to knit among people she knew in town.

Thanks to her charisma and her way of speaking, but above all for her great talent, she managed to get many immigrant people who lived in nearby communities to visit her to ask her to knit something for their babies.

Emma, almost six years of age, excelled at school because of her gift of painting and sculpting beautiful works of art, which earned her several awards in the region.

Despite the fact that she did not speak much, she had a very good repertoire of not very common words that Phillip and Elida taught her at home, as part of the good education she received on mutual respect and kind treatment with people.

We have to remember that good values are learned at home, and that was reflected in little Moonlight in everything she did. She was one of the best students in science, and one of the forerunners to implement meditation for children in school. Unfortunately, like many other things, the idea only gained strength due to the ridicule of some teachers who took it as a joke, when one of the teachers who loved Emma very much proposed the idea to them at a teachers' meeting.

Undoubtedly, the formation and education of our children is based on the political ideas of some individuals who hold power, and not on what they really need so that one day we can be a civilized and prepared society and thus be able to transcend a little more in heavenly justice.

Unfortunately, our children are only prepared to occupy a predetermined position in society, which is suggested by the media that attack freedom of thought. Conditioned to serve the political and social causes that prevail in these times, but not to achieve a unified conscience in a common objective. By integrating a little more into the social life of his peers,

Phillip met many immigrants who worked in the fields and in construction areas, as well as restaurants and many other areas, where some received very bad treatment from their employers to the point of almost treating them like slaves. They were paid less than the minimum wage and forced to work longer hours than the law allowed. Many suffered the disappointment of being discriminated against by their own countrymen, mistreating them and threatening to report them to the immigration service, if they did not obey their terms. All this injustice worried Phillip greatly, that no matter how much he resisted, he could not avoid intervening, to mediate among the confusion that contaminates these poor spirits lacking guidance, lacking love.

He knew that it was impossible for them to listen to him, because he was one more immigrant who had crossed the border illegally, and who also did not have the power to make people change their way of thinking; Well, what could he tell them that they would care to hear, but what this world of injustice has already instilled in their aspirations as members of society.

There he was again, inadvertently falling into the same self-doubt that was holding him back.

Despite trying to warn them about the truth of the spirit in carnal life, he thought that it is best to let people live their lives in their own way, without external interventions that limit the great potential that exists within each and every human being in the universe. And that, furthermore, each one must grow in his own way, among the shadows or confusion, between pain and sorrow, between love and hate.

In time they will understand that our lives were like a distant day in our youth, and of which we only remember a few details. That is not why life is less valuable, but it is part of every day that makes up our time as spirits.

Not wanting to attract the attention of those greedy and corrupted by power, he was content with the apparent peace in which they developed as mere mortals, trying to forget the designs that the divine had placed on them.

Even so, there were details on occasions that reminded Phillip of his obligation as a spirit, having no choice but to intervene in one way or another to help those abused by injustice. Although he did it in the most discreet way possible because this time, he was willing not to risk anyone's life.

Many times, he had to remain silent in the face of injustice, hatred, and indiscriminate racism, not only from the local ignoramuses, but from those whom he considered his countrymen.

One Sunday they met in the town of Glasgow, along with other friends to celebrate the national holidays of their native country. They dressed Emma in a typical costume of the region where they came from, because they were so proud of their ancestral roots. Elida and Phillip were no exception, both dressed in typical costumes to give the celebration more originality.

Many admired their costumes, because they made them feel proud and melancholic at the same time, missing the land that saw them born.

The food was plentiful and from different regions, with different flavors and colors that would appeal to any eye of any nationality.

Typical regional music was played by a band made up of some boys from the community, who liked to get together in their spare time to enjoy jazz and blues music. For now, they only played the Zacatecas march and other melodies that people requested.

Everything was happiness and celebration in that house, where Phillip and his family were very proudly received by their owners, seeing the original outfits they had dressed in.

The owner of the house welcomed them and sat on the right side of his table, where there were only three empty chairs in the house; Well, many people attended the invitation

177

that that family had made to the community, not only to celebrate national holidays; Rather, they jointly celebrated the upcoming arrival of their three children, who at that time had already crossed the border, so they only waited for them to reach the town of Glasgow.

Phillip listened carefully to what Mr. Ponce de León was saying about his children, at the moment he heard a tenor sing to him about a peach tree, in which he was sitting under its shadow next to Elida and Emma. He reminded of the afternoons when his mother warned him about that tenor, which was coming looking for him to the hut to sing to him for a good time, and he came out to listen to it singing.

He almost shed a tear when he remembered his mother, unless he turned to see his loved ones who looked at him with a big smile on their faces, because of the joy they felt sharing such a pleasant experience with others celebration.

They ate enough not to want even one more glass of water, despite the fact that the heat was rather strong that day.

Emma soon made some friends, so she went to play with them some typical games that their parents had taught them.

Phillip felt a sensation in his chest, which made him think of the children of Mr. Ponce de León, almost feeling the anguish that those innocent people felt in the middle of nowhere, walking through a deceitful dream that would not give them the answer that their spirits needed.

Elida was talking with two ladies and a young teenager, about three tables from where Phillip was. She had also felt the sensation at the same time as him, so she turned to look at him immediately as if she was asking him if he knew what was happening. Phillip nodded to her, and she immediately stood up to look for Emma, who was playing with the other children in the back of the house.

A young man ran into the house looking for Mr. Ponce de León, because he had a very urgent message for him. Those

178

who saw the young man enter were a little worried when they saw the scared face he showed. He had to shout by his name to call him out of the crowd. "Don León, don León!" the young man shouted.

Mr. Ponce de León, upon hearing the boy's voice, he recognized him immediately, so he walked quickly towards the boy, hoping to receive news from his children; Well, the boy was the same one who did the errands in the community store, and who always let him know when his children called him from his country. That was the only way to communicate with them, since hardly anyone had a telephone at that time.

Someone had called to tell him that his three children had died in the desert, that they had been found the night before, with signs of having died of thirst and hunger a few days before. The person who spoke to leave the message was the same person who found the phone number written on a piece of paper, in the pocket of one of his children. He had decided to call when he realized that the word above the phone number said: Dad.

Some good people break the conventions of conduct to attend to the heart and take pity on the pain of the poor innocents who suffer the misfortunes with which life teaches us the lessons to grow.

It was thanks to the good heart of that person who warned him about the misfortune that had happened, so he was able to find out about the death of his children. So, he could at least have the privilege of burying them with dignity. Since, on countless occasions, many die trying to reach the north, and not even traces of their bones have been found. This is the end of many of our brothers and sisters, for seeking the dream of being able to give their loved ones a better future, without knowing that it would cost them their lives.

Without a doubt, that was a very bitter day for everyone in the house of Mr. Ponce de León, who even the ones who hardly knew him approached him to offer their condolences and support him in whatever he needed. Trying to cheer him up anyway, no one found a way that would ease the pain in his heart.

Ponce de León fell to his knees asking heaven why it had taken them.

"Weren't they good?" — Ponce de León was torn asking heaven.

Phillip approached him and put his hand on his forehead, to show him a little of our creator's designs. Ponce de León did not stop crying or reproaching heaven for his loss, despite the fact that Phillip tried to show him what he knew. For some strange reason, his power did not work with that man, because he was drowned in tears, and his voice went from reproaching heaven so much for having taken away his loved ones.

Elida approached him and gave him a big hug, which brought a bit of calm to that man, who had lost not only what he loved most in life, but even his faith.

People withdrew from the party, some to go back to their homes due to the sadness of what had happened, and some indifferent went to find a place to continue celebrating, not being part of the pain that burned the heart of Ponce de León.

Emma, seeing the pain the man was in, approached him and placed her hand on his heart. That man passed the bitterness that hurt his throat when he felt the warmth of love that came from Emma's hand, so at that moment he hugged her and asked her to forgive him, but to understand his pain. Little Moonlight kissed him on the cheek and said something in his ear. Ponce de León looked at her in astonishment, as if he was frightened to hear Emma's words.

The crying stopped and hope returned to his face, which had been lost due to the rancor and hatred that such a misfortune had caused him. Phillip and Elida offered him

180

their friendship, and promised to visit him often so he would not feel abandoned. That he could trust them, and if there was anything they could do for him. Mr. Ponce de León thanked them with all his heart for wanting to comfort him, although he warned them that this would be something very difficult to achieve, because he could not accept that God had taken away his children, after asking him every night for many years to give him the privilege of being able to see them again. There was no way to comfort him.

Phillip met a young man who lived in that town on that same occasion, who worked fixing the roofs of the houses, and who, after having talked for a long time with him, realized the personality with which Phillip demonstrated his humility when give his opinion on some things, and he did not hesitate to invite him to work with his working group.

Phillip talked to Elida about what his friend named Antonio Nieves had offered him.

Antonio told him that he had a house where they could stay, but that it was in the town of Bowling Green, Kentucky. About half an hour from where he lived. That he should not worry, since they worked in different parts of the state fixing the roofs of houses, he would pick him up in the morning to go to work.

Elida told him that the best thing she could do was follow him wherever he wanted. To count on her for anything, but to take in consideration the stability they already had, as well as the goodwill of her friends in Hendersonville, by offering them their house for as long as they needed it.

Phillip spoke with his friend Julio to tell him what he planned to do, and to thank him for how much he had helped them, for which he told him that if he needed his help in the future, he should not hesitate to look for it.

They had already formed a great friendship, so it was difficult for them to say goodbye. Especially for Emma, who was very happy with her friends, whom she could not resign herself to not being able to see often. Phillip promised her that he would bring her back to town from time to time, so that she could see her friends. That she should not be sad because she would not abandon them forever.

They lived in Bowling Green until Emma was six and a half, and where they settled to try to live the dream that not many manage to achieve, a happy and free home to live life with dignity.

Phillip found a job at a frozen food packinghouse in the Delafield area because work to fix the roofs had stopped for the winter. Antonio told him that he could stay in the house as long as he thought necessary, because the roofing would be good after spring, so it was good that he worked somewhere else during that time.

The place where he worked at the packing house was about two blocks from the house that Antonio had let them stay in. It seemed that there was a certain fortune at times that benefited him; Well, he had a house to live in, as well as being able to walk to work without any problem.

Many immigrants suffer from the need for transportation to go to work every day, having to depend on the goodwill of others to be able to go out and find their daily bread. Sometimes the price for the ride was unfair, but one had to put up with pride very often, there was no other way.

It is sad to realize the abuse by those whom we believe are our peers, or our countrymen. But worse is living the discrimination and ingratitude of these naive misguided, who believe they have some privilege over the poor and innocent.

Emma, as always, excelled at her new school, where she found new friends with whom to share the good times of childhood, and which will undoubtedly never return. Unfortunately, just like many of our immigrant children, little Moonlight suffered from the discrimination and racism that plagues the innocent lives of children in this nation. It was thanks to her great example that her parents gave her that she

182

was able to overcome the unjustified mockery by these poor ignorant and deceived people. On some occasions they tried to physically assault her when their absurd taunts were unsuccessful, which caused more anger in these poor ignoramuses when they realized that they could not hurt her with their stupidity, since she always ignored them. Little Emma told her parents what was happening to her at school, that even on weekends at lunchtime she always prayed for those rude children, because she thought that perhaps those children were not happy at home.

On Thursday afternoons she had singing lessons with the church choir, while Phillip took advantage of the time to take some piano lessons. After all, he had to wait an hour while the kids practiced their singing lessons.

With what Elida taught him and what young Mathew managed to do, so that he would continue on his way to learn to play the piano decently like any other musician in the field, just as his mother always wanted him to do. Phillip, thinking precisely about that, decided to continue with the lessons.

Young Mathew, who was his piano instructor, and who attended Hillvue church regularly, was only eighteen years old when he was teaching Phillip the musical scales. He was a nice young man with a very good heart, who always offered to help in what his time allowed, since he had to attend school in the morning, and in the afternoon, he volunteered at church. Despite the fact that it was just a basement where some people met, it was a place where they could breathe the hope for peace that they so needed in their lives.

Thanks to the great effort and willingness to learn, it was that Phillip came to have the privilege of accompanying the church choir in some praises and songs. He always bragged about those moments, because he said that he experienced an inexplicable ecstasy when expressing with music what he felt. It was thanks to the fact that the church community welcomed them with their affection and acceptance that they were able to overcome the discrimination they often suffered for being different from the rest of the town's population. They treated them as their fellow men, as their brothers in spirit.

On Sunday afternoons he liked to take his loved ones to Wilkerson Island, to have a good time with nature.

He had rebuilt an old waltz that was found on the banks of the Barren River, with wood from fallen logs that he collected near the shore, which he pulled out with the help of Elida and little Moonlight, with a rope that he had made himself of materials that was always among the things that other people no longer wanted. They spent countless moments together walking paths and places that very few appreciated, living deceived in the false idea of reality. For Phillip and for his loved ones, deception never took over their dreams or their beliefs, because the strength of their spirit was stronger than any greed or foolishness. There was no way the confusion would surprise them, or that corruption or fear imprisoned them among their countless cells of vanity or ego. They were happy despite the indifference and injustice with which the world treated them.

It is a pity that the world does not give a damn about the good ideals, or the good intentions of our hearts.

On one occasion when he decided to go to the river alone, because he had a feeling that there might be a thunderstorm that day, he decided to fish under the bridge on the road to Richardville, since catfish tend to hide among the logs that were piled up under the bridge.

Almost before nightfall, among the flushed and magical light with which the universe bids farewell to the day, he looked at a young couple who were arguing inside the car in which they were traveling. They had stopped halfway across the bridge so they could shout their arguments as loudly as possible. Neither accepted the possibility of being wrong; on the contrary, they shouted their reproaches in each other's faces. Without any clarity in the fuss they were having because they were talking like turkeys.

At the end of the bridge, at the very top of the structure that had just parted from the sunlight, he saw a strange creature, very dull gray in color, with eyes redder than a ruby, and wings larger than those of a Golden Eagle.

Phillip realized that he was stalking that couple who were arguing in the middle of the bridge, and he tried to warn them by yelling at them that a being alien to this world was stalking them. Their own shouts of mutual reproach prevented them from hearing Phillip's, who was trying to warn them about this strange creature. Phillip hastened to row as close as he could to the structure of the bridge, to climb up and try to help those innocents who were misunderstanding each other in pride.

When he was halfway to get to where the couple was, he heard the screams of terror from the young woman; and in an instant he saw the young man with a broken neck fall into the river and got lost in the current. He hurried up as fast as he could, but when he got to the top of the bridge, he realized it was too late.

That creature had destroyed the young woman also, and was trying to take her away, because it was tying her up with some kind of dark green rope with dried blood stains everywhere.

Phillip stared into its eyes, without stopping the creature from its intention to tie her properly to take her away. Immediately his memories invaded him with some fury, when he remembered his mother's tears that afternoon when she rescued him almost from the black bird's clutches. Certainly, looked like the same hellish creature.

He was not afraid of wanting to face that beast foreign to this world, nor did he doubt even for an instant his capacity as the chosen one. Although he did not quite understand what was happening. The creature made a strange sound, which reminded Phillip of the sound alligators make at night when they sail up the Mississippi.

He put his hand into his backpack to touch the book, so the creature dropped the young woman to the ground and enraged by the energy that the book generated Phillip, it bellowed full of rage and began to back away.

At the moment it tried to take flight, with one of its legs it took the end of the rope, and when it rose, it threw the young woman into the river so that the current would carry her away. It disappeared into the clouds, just like the creature that had tried to take him as a child.

The young woman had been stuck between the logs where Phillip had tried to fish a few minutes before the tragedy.

Suddenly he realized that he had been dreaming, because he had fallen asleep in the raft, fishing for the catfish that hide among the logs that are piled up under the bridge. Puzzled and not sure what had happened, he wondered if this was some sign or warning.

The sun had already set, but the amber color of a distant sunset still remained, which dismissed the day and ushered in night, so that we hasten to return to the same place from which we arose.

He turned back as soon as he could to get home before the night got darker. Even thinking about the peculiarity of his vision, without specifying exactly if that had happened in some remote time, or that perhaps it would happen at some point in the future.

The sea of thought that occupied his reality made him not worry about what commonly happened to him, about those inconclusive and imprecise visions that warned him of things that were never entirely clear to him. However, he still kept thinking about those malevolent eyes, the same eyes that he remembered from when he was a child.

He came home just with a fish that was not a very good size, and even Elida asked him why he had not left it back in the river. He replied that what one proposed was not always achieved, that sometimes one should accept what the universe put in their hands, because, even if it was a small fish, at least they would have something to eat. She understood it perfectly, being a humble woman with a good heart. She approached him and told him that he was absolutely right, because the universe is never wrong or backs down. On the contrary, it provides what the spirit needs to grow one step closer to our creator.

In the end they decided to grill it on the coals along with two other fish that he had caught the day before, with some potatoes and onions, plus some roasted jalapeno peppers for extra flavor.

Phillip was trying to watch the soccer game on a small television that his friend Antonio Nieves had given him, at the moment when Elida and Emma were playing in front of the television, so they did not let him clearly see the moment when Paolo Rossi scored a spectacular headed goal against Argentina. Phillip was a bit upset for not having been able to see that goal clearly, so he asked them to lower the noise a bit and calm down from running from here to there, because they did not let him hear the narration of the game.

"Let us be, don't be bitter, Quixote." Elida told him, at the moment that she hugged Moonlight.

Elida held her while the little girl screamed to let her go. But then Emma asked her to teach her again how to get away quickly if someone tried to take her by force. He only contemplated them thinking about how right her beloved was when she tried to teach Moonlight how to defend herself from the evil ones. Although sometimes there is no way to escape their injustices, nor their lies.

Phillip decided to go out to check the fish that they had on the coals, in a small stove that he built with some stones, on which he placed a grill that he found from an old barbecue. The fish were just right, the onions and jalapeño peppers smelled delicious, so he decided to take them out and put them on a tray he had found, which could well be over a hundred years old, but Phillip liked it for the theme he had of some peacocks on the deck.

He decided to return inside the house to have dinner to his loved ones and celebrate dinner together.

Suddenly he noticed a strange blue light that was positioned above the house, so he rushed to enter quickly, even knocking the tray with food to the ground.

Looking out the window, he saw Elida and Moonlight in the kitchen still laughing for the joy that was simply born from their hearts, without realizing what was happening.

Phillip froze, thinking that perhaps he was having a vision, just at the moment when the kitchen ceiling was opened by the force of the blue light, from where four reptilian-like humanoid creatures descended.

Two took Elida and one took Emma, to tie them up and cover their mouths so they would stop screaming. Phillip reacted immediately to try to do something, but he could not open the door. It seemed as if time was not the same. As if nothing was real.

Knowing that anything was possible and understanding the nature of his mission as protector of the truth, he hurried back to open the door.

When he finally knocked it down, he rushed inside to prevent them from being taken away, but it was too late, from the moment he opened the door, these cold-blooded beings were rising into the air, taking his loved ones with them. He managed to hear some sounds that these reptiles made, which he thought would be their language. Among those sounds he clearly heard that one of those creatures mentioned a person's name. That would be the only clue that they left behind after they banished.

The hours passed and he never stopped crying because of the anguish he felt after losing them, because of the pain in his chest when he felt that the vision was beginning to materialize.

For the first time in a long time, he was afraid that he could not save them. He reproached himself for having caused such misfortune to the beings he loved the most in life, for which he prayed to heaven to free his family and take him instead. But the silence only made his crying turn to bitterness.

The dawn seemed insignificant to him, sad and empty without the presence of his loved ones.

He could not even sleep for a moment, because he was thinking and trying to remember the visions that could help him, to explain what had happened to his family, and how to rescue them from those loveless creatures. Pain did not let him think right, nor could he find the reason for what had happened. He could not believe or accept that they were no longer by his side. He cried until he lost hope and conscience in the midst of the misery he became without them.

He did not go to work for the next three days, trying to meditate enough to find some answer within himself that would illuminate the darkness of helplessness he felt when he could not do anything.

While trying to remember what had happened that night, he had a vision of some details that he had not noticed because he was desperate trying to open the door. He remembered that they would be taken to the moon, according to what the leader of the creatures had said as they rose into the air.

He had to meditate on it very well to not be mistaken, thinking that perhaps he was going crazy imagining all this, for trying to find a logical answer where only fantasy seemed to reign.

It took him a lot of work to accept that this was what had happened, and much more to accept that it was actually possible that his loved ones were really on the moon. Every night he looked at the moon thinking that his loved ones would be there waiting for him to rescue them. And he remembered the visions that he had had about the calls for help that he heard sometimes at night, which came from the moon, according to his intuition. He understood that the visions were focused on that moment, and that the calls were those of his loved ones. He fell to his knees and cried, screaming helplessly because of the pain he felt in his chest, not having the way to rescue them from the tyranny that had kidnapped them.

A representative from the Warren County School Board visited the house to find out why Emma had not attended school on those days.

She found Phillip lying on the ground crying out of despair at not knowing what to do. She asked him about Emma and his wife Elida that if she could talk to them. Phillip slowly got up stammering a few meaningless words, then he stared at her without knowing what to say; Well, what could he tell her to make her believe the fantastic reason why she could not talk to them. "I don't know where they are." Philip answered.

The school representative looked at him desperately crying without having slept in days, which made her feel sorry for the misery he became without his loved ones. She asked him again the reason why Elida and Emma were not in the house, but Phillip did not know what to say.

The lady suspected that something strange was happening, so she asked him what he had done to them, to tell her where they were, or she would go to the police to report them missing. There was no logical answer that he could give her, so Phillip only remained silent, thinking about what fate had in store for him.

He was arrested for being suspected of having murdered his wife and daughter, in addition to other charges that were put on him by the prosecutor, who was a rude and

190

unprincipled guy, and who also did not like immigrants very much. They assigned a novice to plead for him, who was also the judge's son.

The only thing that Phillip declared was that he did not know where they were, and that he had not murdered them. He did not know how to explain to them what had happened that night, in which they were kidnapped by those cold-blooded creatures.

They tried to make him confess in every possible way, that even the lawyer tried to persuade him to confide in him where the bodies were, since he was the one defending him, he could manage to help him get free. Phillip was aware of the absurd intentions on the part of these men, who only sought to blame him.

The judge had planned everything to make him talk about the whereabouts of his daughter and his wife, as a strategy to frame him one way or another.

By not pleading guilty or finding any evidence of the whereabouts of Elida and Emma, the prosecutor and the judge agreed to charge him with other crimes, so that he could not get out of jail until they found the bodies.

The lawyer told him that the charges he had were very serious, that he had better declare the truth so that he would not have any more problems. Phillip decided to tell them everything that had happened.

The prosecutor and the judge, as well as the police chief and two detectives were behind the glass where Phillip was declaring the events that had happened that night.

The police chief got very angry, arguing that Phillip was a deranged madman, that there was no doubt that he was delirious in a fanciful story to hide his misdeeds.

The prosecutor and the judge supported him with the same attitude, except for the two detectives who only turned to see each other from time to time, when listening to the story that Phillip said about what had happened to his family.

The truth does not always set you free, especially if your captors are partakers of lies or ignorance. Phillip was aware of this, who understood that no man would dare to help him knowing the nature of the disappearance of his family, because anyone would think that this was an invented or imagined madness. That made him lose hope of being able to do anything to rescue them. Although that seemed like an impossible thing to achieve, since there are no means to even attempt it.

They decided to do a polygraph test to make sure he was lying and blame him for the death of his family. But the results only confused the authorities because they found no trace that he was lying.

The judge and the prosecutor did not willingly accept the results presented by the two detectives, who demanded Phillip's release due to lack of compelling evidence.

In the end, to not letting him go free, despite the fact that the results were negative, the judge and the prosecutor took him to trial, but they reluctantly accepted that the polygraph results be used as evidence in his favor. An unnecessary trial since the evidence showed that he was not lying. The two detectives made sure that his rights were respected, despite being undocumented.

Somehow the news of the statement appeared in the local newspaper, which followed Phillip's case for the disappearance of Elida and Emma, causing people's attention due to the strangeness of the news. "A girl and her mother are abducted by aliens!" the newspaper headline read.

The authorities disagreed with Phillip's statements, and insisted that they were just crazy things invented, which reflected how sick he was.

The news spread faster than the plague, so it reached the ears of those who are interested in issues related to this matter. Not only those who govern in the most tabloid way possible, but also those who control the media to make us forget certain details about ourselves. Each one judge in your own way.

Six days after the verdict, after several months of procedures and investigations, he received a visit from a very tall young man with a very subtle appearance, who began to question him about what he had said in his statement.

Phillip realized the energy that this young man radiated with his presence, and his impeccable black suit that he was wearing caught his attention. He told him what happened, trusting that he was doing the right thing.

He felt an energy that subjected him against the wall, at the moment when the young man pointed his hand at him. He told him that he should not say another word on the subject, otherwise, he would kill him like a cockroach. He would get him out of jail with that one condition, that he declare it was a fabrication for not knowing where his family was. That he said that because stress had caused him to invent so many crazy things. This time, the prosecutor and the judge were the only ones behind the mirror. Phillip declared that he had invented everything because of the confusion he felt that perhaps someone else had kidnapped his family.

The rumors calmed down with Phillip's statement, but they brought controversy because they had not found traces of the whereabouts of Elida and Emma anywhere.

The media took it upon themselves to make the news become a joke, to hide the clues that would guide men towards the truth of their own condition in this world, in which freedom is bought with lies about promises of hate and racial discrimination, for interests that the Elites invent in their favor to deceive the people.

Phillip was released free of charge, but with the only restriction of not being able to leave town, thanks to the fact that the police chief insisted on the judge and the prosecutor applying the travel ban. He walked from the courthouse along the Main Avenue towards the Barren River, but decided to take Church Avenue, so that he could reach the Delafield area sooner. He stopped for a moment on one of the steps of the San José Church, to get some air and strength, because they had not given him food in jail for a couple of days.

Suddenly he felt the presence of The Old Lady with the White Hair, who warned him that he should enter the chapel as soon as possible because his life was in danger if he stayed one more minute sitting on the steps. Phillip did not doubt for an instant that warning, so he immediately ran into the chapel.

At that moment, and without anyone noticing where they had come from, a gang of hateful criminals passed by throwing gasoline bottles at the church and shouting obscene words against their beliefs. Breaking windows and knocking down fences, those deceived by the lies of their petty leader boasted with their rancor. Phillip could only protect himself from the savage aggression of the deceived and ignorant, who wanted to burn down the church.

When the deceived finally left, all the neighbors joined Phillip's effort to put out the flames, which those poor ignoramuses had caused with their arrogance and hatred. The parish priest and two other priests helped the altar boy carry water in some buckets, to put out some flames that were spreading into the chapel.

Phillip closed his eyes, and suddenly the doors were opened by a strong wind that extinguished the flames in an instant, so everyone stayed for a few seconds wondering what had happened. But with the confusion and fear, no one realized the peculiarity of the details, nor Phillip's intention to help keep the chapel safe. Except for one of the priests who was nearby, who could see when Phillip with the strength of his spirit put out the fire of hatred and resentment.

Seeing the firemen arrive to help put down the latest blazes of hate, he was pleased that he was able to help save the church from the fire, and he left without anyone even noticing he was ever there. He had more sorrows to attend to, and impossible missions to try to solve.

The loneliness at home did not bring him logical answers that would give him a reason that he could use to alleviate the pain of not having his family by his side, because he could not bear the idea of them being with those loveless creatures, who they would surely be murdered without any mercy.

Three days after not being able to sleep thinking about how to look for his loved ones, six immigration agents arrived at his house around nine in the morning. They demanded that the door be opened for them, or else they would throw it down. Phillip immediately opened the door asking what was going on.

The immigration officers asked for his name to confirm that he was on the list, so one of them only said yes when Phillip told them his name. The other two officers then threw him to the ground and beat him nearly unconscious. Then they handcuffed him and dragged him to the truck, where they brought others who had already checked their list.

Almost unconscious and with one eye half closed, he could see the sad faces of those poor immigrants who suffered the same fate as him.

He could not say anything for a few minutes because the officials threatened them to keep quiet, or else they would show them who was in charge in that land. According to the words of the immigration officers. The others suggested to him, making a sign with their hands, to not say a word.

For some strange divine reason, they did not take his backpack, so he put his hand on top of the book. That gave him some relief, knowing that all was not lost.

By the will of that same strange force that allowed him to take the book with him, it was that he was able to tell others not to lose their faith, because the divine ones would surely deal with the wicked and ignorant in due time, since no wickedness remains unanswered to divine justice.

They were taken to the town of Leitchfield for a few days, then transferred to Chicago, from where they would be transported to the McAllen border a month later; so that they could be deported to their country of origin.

Phillip would have never imagined such cruelty on the part of the officers who abused the immigrants, beating and insulting them miserably and without any human consideration. He never imagined the injustice or the hatred that was reflected in the faces of those haughty people, nor the petty aggressions they made against the innocent and defenseless.

Now he realized how serious the deception was, and how impossible it seemed that one day he could help them to free themselves from the lie in which they were condemned. He felt a deep pity for those unfortunate deceived, knowing that they would inevitably suffer the payment for their misdeeds, without mercy or comfort.

On one of those nights, he heard that an officer was raping a young woman in one of the offices of the facility where they were being held prisoners. No one dared to say a single word because they were afraid of these abusers.

The very miserable rapist took the young woman back to her cell, all bloody from her face, crying inconsolably asking him not to hit her anymore. Silence was the only thing that made that young woman stop crying, resigning herself to her miserable fate as a poor immigrant in this nation, which they call "The land of the free"

Phillip wept inconsolably at the injustice and arrogance of those mere mortals who played at being gods. He reproached himself for not having brought the medallion and the pectoral with him, because with it he could surely do something in the face of so much evil. Again, he thought of using The Tools of Order to end the iniquitous and ignorant, who did not show any sign of being civilly capable of upholding good or justice.

The book gave him the necessary strength and good sense not to fall into the mistaken idea that rancor and hatred were causing him.

He tried his best not to succumb to the injustice and ignorance with which they were treated. Above all, he had to be strong not to lose his sanity, because he knew that he still had a long way to go before trying to save his loved ones.

That day they were taken to the border to be deported, a large crowd dressed in white protested to demand justice and dignity for immigrants.

In the wall that the separatists built, they left a few gates along the border to control full access to the country.

The black door was opened for immigrants to cross back to their homeland. Among them was Phillip walking with great difficulty because of the beating that immigration officers had given him almost daily before he went to bed, for the simple fact of being different.

Phillip fell to his knees remembering the night his loved ones had been kidnapped by those creatures out of this world, at the precise moment when the crowd coming from every town and nation could be seen on the other side of the black door, which was closed behind Phillip, who was on his knees on the ground remembering his loved ones. They protested with posters and banners, which shouted the words that fools often ignore due to lack of human integrity and love for their neighbor.

_jema_sid

Duality

The night ended with different surprises, but at the same time everything falls into the simplicity of the banal.

I sense how it manipulates the passionate minds of its innocent puppets, unconscious creatures of their condition.

One by one it link in its evil plot in search of the end, in the overflowing dramas of their lives, with fury and hatred, and naivety.

It is coming after me, screwing up my life.

In the distance I see the dust raised by the hooves of their horses, and their riders raising their axes to slit my throat.

That suffocating dust of hellish condition are the dramas of these creatures.

Incapable of understanding their state, they passionately live their frantic search for happiness.

It gets into the eyes and there is no way to avoid it, because it penetrates deep into the luminous dust of dreams.

The ears are susceptible, and our state too.

I no longer know what is natural, or what has been created by this society, this race of pain and hate.

Generation of indifferent and selfish, individualists lacking in understanding.

The conscious are few, but even so, they fall for its dramas, and it pursues them in its evil machination to the end.

Just like all this dusty legion of anguish and resentment, there is also one in the divine that instructs and guides us.

It gives us the understanding and preparation to face the battle.

And conspire in favor, even in the dark. It is the gentle light of reason, the silence of His voice and the magic of His everything.

9/4/2009